BESPELLED

SPELLBOUND SERIES

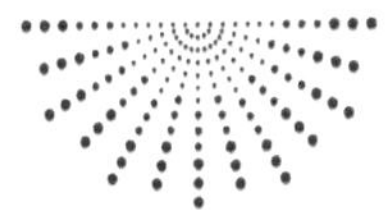

DANI KRISTOFF

v

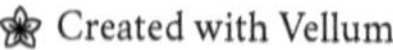 Created with Vellum

To the magic of love

CHAPTER ONE

Sydney Harbor filled Jake Royston's line of sight as he gazed out the 35th floor window of the AMP building near Circular Quay. The 180-degree view showed a cruise ship at berth near The Rocks, and ferries making their way out of the quay to Manly and further afield. A forty-foot yacht, its prow cutting deep, made its way toward the heads. The boat passed out of sight, its passage cut off by the white sails of the Opera House.

For a moment, Jake wished he was out there, lapping up the sun and sea, but he let the thought float away. He had more important things to do.

'Yes, I got that,' he said into the phone, making a note in the file in front of him. 'My assistant will get back to you shortly.' He listened, as his client pressed him. 'She'll confirm a meeting time today.' He cut off the connection and buzzed through to his executive assistant. 'Pen, set up a meeting tomorrow with the Stanton Brothers. They're getting cold feet. I need to seal the deal before it sours.'

'You have space on Monday. Is that soon enough?'

Jake buried his forehead in his hands. 'You can't fit them in?'

'Only if I reschedule someone else. Saturday is getting pretty full.'

Jake switched the screen over to his schedule. The Stanton brothers might be getting twitchy, but their case was not as urgent as some of the others. 'Jake?'

'Okay. It'll have to do.' Jake's finger aimed for the intercom cut-off button.

'Before you go, you asked me to remind you about cocktails this evening — the Lowton's product launch.'

Jake sighed. 'Thanks for the reminder. I forgot all about it.'

'Do you want me to confirm Krista as your date?'

Jake sat back and rubbed his chin. Krista was blonde, voluptuous and a long-legged beauty. Her mind was on one thing: landing a husband with lots of money. 'Sure. Tell her I said to wear red.'

He cut off the intercom and grinned. She'd wear black to show she was an independent woman. No way was he was falling for her lures, though. His heart was armored up, good and proper.

Love had done nothing for his father. Three un-lucky marriages, all in the name of love, and all the old man had now was a third of his fortune and a small flat in Mosman.

Luckily, Jake always had a good supply of ad-mirers so he never went without sex, and was never denied when he had to ask instead of having it dished up to him. That was the life for him — all pleasure, and no commitment. At thirty two, he had done everything he'd set out to achieve, and he'd managed to keep his body in good shape while studying the long hours it took to get his degree. He had a certain charm that had helped him along in his career. It had to be charm rather than luck, given some of the deals he'd managed to pull off. He was good at persuading people. It was as natural for him as breathing.

He flicked through his account file listing, and frowned at an old case. He gritted his teeth and buzzed through to Pen.

'Have we heard from Grace Riordon yet?' That particular party had been grating on his nerves for some time.

'An email arrived from her about ten minutes ago. It's in your inbox.'

Jake chewed his bottom lip as he read the message, raising his eyebrow. 'Now she wants to talk?' he muttered. *Sending a representative...a cousin...can speak for her.* Excellent. It was about time.

Jake reached into his desk drawer and pulled out the account file. *Last piece of land before the development can proceed... Two years negotiating with the Riordon party.* He read the email again. Looks like the cousin was going to contact him today. He'd chew her up and spit her out. Some accounts get stuck in one's craw, and this Riordon business had pushed him too far. The deal should have been finalized eighteen months ago. It was costing his client. Jake would get paid either way, but the delay made him look bad.

Pen walked in, coffee in one hand, and the newspaper in the other. She was short, dark haired, had a cute button nose, and freckles smattered under her big blue eyes. They'd known each other since university, but had only ever been friends. That relationship suited him fine, because she took everything he dished out and there were no love complications.

'Here you go, boss. You didn't pick up your paper and I think you need this.' She handed over the espresso. The aroma teased his nostrils. He scowled. He didn't want her to think he'd gone soft. Taking a long draw of the coffee, he knew straight away Pen had gone to Bella Café, where the espresso was always fine.

'You read my mind,' he said gruffly, and took another sip. 'About the cocktail party. What's the latest we can hold off confirming attendance?'

Pen threw her dark ponytail over her shoulder. 'I'm not sure, but I'll find out. You could say you're sick, or that you hurt your back doing weights.' She looked him up and down. 'You're way too buff to be legal.'

'It's too early in the morning for sass.' He took another sip of coffee and closed his eyes. 'Back to this evening — '

'You want me to cancel the date with Krista.'

'Yes,' he replied, looking at her askance. The way she read him was unnerving. 'You can substitute for her if I'm desperate.'

Pen laughed as she walked away. 'Sorry, I have a hot date, so no deal.' She closed the door and then poked her head back in the room. 'Shall I send Krista flowers by way of apology?'

'What for? We're not exclusive. She'll get another date. Don't you worry.'

Pen's dark eyebrows drew down. 'I gave up worrying about you a long time ago, Heart-of-Stone Jake Royston. A dart from Cupid's arrow would bounce off your steel-coated heart and shatter.'

Jake chuckled, amused by Pen's needling. What was it with assistants these days? They want to be your therapist and organize your life. *Sheez.* 'If you hear from...' He checked the email. '...Elena Denholm, agree to whatever she suggests regarding a meeting. Make sure she meets with me today. I want this deal sealed.'

'It will have to be after five. You're meeting Mrs

Coulston at four thirty. Her case is pending, so she can't be put off.'

He nodded, checking his computer for the Coulston file. Pen shut the door, leaving Jake to sip coffee and lose himself in case notes.

E lena Denholm finished the plait on her herb charm, yanking it tight to remove a kink. She admired her handiwork; lovely fresh raffia braided together with dried flowers, herbs, colorful ribbon and magic-infused trinkets. Her magic was gentle, light and beneficial. She reached up, standing on tip-toes to secure the final ribbon, in which she placed a spell that would exude calmness and contentment — the perfect precondition for a healthy life.

As she stood back, she lifted her gaze to the chin-up bar she used when preparing her charms and nodded to herself. The old gym equipment she'd bought in a garage sale had proved useful for making the long, graceful charms.

Her human customers didn't really question why her charms made them feel good. Some of her most committed customers were other members of the folk, witches, warlocks and fairies, who could make their own. That didn't stop them from buying her charms for themselves, their families and friends.

With the final batch ready for the markets, she packed them ready for sale. She sighed as she placed the last charm into the display basket.

Elena was a half-witch. Her mother had never spilled the beans to her relatives on who her father was. Aunt Elvira always said he was a human and her cousin, Grace, who she had lived with since she was thirteen, had made up an amazing array of fanciful tales about who her father was and what he did. She had theories that he was an airline pilot, a prince, a football star, the president — you name it, Grace had made a story up about it. All the stories had been hilarious and involved very convoluted scenarios that usually sent the listener into breathless laughing fits. Elena smiled at the remembrance. All the laughing they did had helped her cope with not knowing her parents, and made her love her adopted family deeply.

A smile lit up her face. Those teenage years with Grace and Aunt Elvira had been happy. It was how she had been brought into the coven and learnt of her witch heritage. Aunt Elvira hadn't been too pleased with her mother for birthing Elena away from the coven, hiding her from her extended family, and having her to a human father. Elena didn't remember her mother at all.

Her phone rang, clanging into her thoughts. It was Grace. No magical power was needed to tell that. Her phone was programmed with that ringtone whenever Grace called.

'Hello, Gracie,' she said, airily.

'Elena, er…hi.'

'What is it? Trouble? Declan?'

Declan Mallory was Grace's gorgeous partner. He'd recently bought a Harley, and both Grace and Elena fretted that he'd have an accident.

'No, Declan's fine. He's visiting his folks up in the Blue Mountains.'

Luckily for Grace, Declan was not only stunningly handsome but a warlock, too. No intermingling issues there. And they'd known each other since childhood. Too bad good warlocks were hard to find in their coven. The pickings were very slim, as Elena had found, to her own disappointment. The sandbox was not big enough to make mistakes in, either.

'I need a favor. You know that development I was telling you about last week?'

Elena nodded and suppressed a groan. Grace didn't like the real world — well, the human one. She couldn't and wouldn't deal with it. Whereas Elena could as she had lived with humans before coming to live with her aunt, within the coven. Dealing with them was as natural to her as casting a spell or weaving a charm.

Elena nodded her head absently. 'Go on.'

'The development company are requesting that I negotiate before they get a court order to force the sale. It appears my block is the only one stopping the development.'

'I thought you weren't going to back down.'

'I wasn't, but the other three landholders who were holding out gave in. Mama says I should drive a hard bargain. I don't really want to lose the land, but if I have to then they should give me a good price. Abide by certain conditions.'

With the phone to her ear, Elena paced the room. *I should wash that dirty coffee cup in the sink.* 'So what can I do, if you have made up your mind?'

'I haven't made up my mind. But I have given you permission to negotiate for me. Please say you will.'

Elena let out a big sigh. 'Really, do I have to?' She wandered to the window and peered through the curtains. It was a lovely day outside, and the gerberas in her garden were a very bright pink.

'You have to meet with their attorney.'

Elena dropped the curtain and her smile. 'What?'

'Some big shot named Jake Royston.'

'But I haven't got experience negotiating with attorneys, big shots or no.'

'I've sent you an email with my negotiating position and his contact details.'

'But, Gracie…I have to prepare for the markets.'

Gracie giggled. 'No, you don't. Mama has already picked your charms up. We'll handle the stall for you.

'Make sure Royston agrees to my conditions. I don't want more pollution making the neighborhood rank.'

She stuck her head in the guest room. There was nothing there but the spare bed and the chrome chin-up bar. 'You've outwitted me again.'

'Before you go…'

'Yes,' she answered, though with less enthusiasm. If Aunt Elvira was there with Grace then she knew what was coming. Family pressure, and all that.

'Have you thought of dating Drew again? Giving him another chance?'

'No.' Penderton — what a disaster that had been. No chemistry, and he was downright surly. 'I believe he doesn't want to see me again, either.'

'Come on, I know the date was a bit of a disaster but…'

'No, Gracie. No. We rub each other the wrong way. His ideas are totally alien to me about everything: magic, women and humans. No deal.'

'But you know his father is real keen.'

'I'm not dating his father, either. There are other witches that will suit him, I'm sure.'

'Elena…'

'Gee, look at the time. I have to go. Love you. Bye.'

Elena flopped down on the sofa. What a close call. She'd been on one date to satisfy them all, and it had been the one date to end them all. She shivered at the memory. It wasn't that he'd done anything bad. It was a vibe thing. Well the vibe, the way he looked, moved, gestured and spoke. When they went on that date, she'd almost been physically ill when he'd tried to kiss her. Not that she admitted that to her family, or anyone in the coven.

She'd rather be single than take Drew Penderton for a spouse, and no amount of cajoling or convincing was going to change her mind. If there was a folk-specific sperm bank, she'd queue up when the time was right.

Managing a child on her own couldn't be that hard. Maybe that would get them off her back. It wasn't like the coven was concerned for her happiness. It was the vacant womb and the declining folk population that concerned them. They needed more witches and warlocks to keep the balance within the folk, and to not disappear completely into the human population.

Even with that pressure, there was no way was she going to settle for a relationship that, well, wasn't a relationship, but an arrangement. She wanted more: love, companionship and passion.

She opened her email and found all the information she needed from Grace. A quick look at the time and, with luck, she could get Jake Royston out of her hair before the end of the day. Life would resume its normality and she'd be free to work her stall in the morning.

The Friday ferry timetable was in her favour. She could catch the Balmain ferry to Circular Quay with plenty of time to spare.

It took a bit of negotiating when she called Royston's, but she managed to secure an appointment for early evening and readily agreed to the suggestion of the Hotel Vive his executive assistant made.

Meeting on neutral territory should work in her favour. He'd probably ride roughshod all over her, and steer his corporate lawyer mojo through her negotiating position. However she wasn't going to give in easily.

After rereading Grace's email, she thought maybe he would take her seriously. Grace's proposal was a very good deal all round. Her cousin might not like dealing with the real world, but she certainly had the chops for it. Jake Royston would be an idiot for not going for it.

It was up to Elena to cinch the deal tight. No magic was to be involved, though. That would be un-ethical. The folk had to live with humans by not taking advantage of them. The use of magic was tightly regulated. Even her charms were only certi-fied for sale to humans after approval by the coven.

After putting the printout of the email into her purse, she turned her attention to getting ready. She'd shower, put on a nice dress, and maybe even some make-up. She needed to look a professional and no-nonsense sort of woman to pull this off. As she rarely went out, she had no power suits, and only a handful of elegant dresses and skirts.

Elena dressed in a knee-length, wraparound dress that split nicely in the front, giving a glimpse of her thigh. Made of forest green fabric, it had a pattern of leaves along the hem. Her breasts were nicely framed by the crossover design. She had nearly gone for button up to the throat demure, but thought she may as well use all her available assets.

Around her throat hung a charm that had been with her since childhood—a charm of protection, made in the image of the goddess, carved in wood. It was the kind of charm that parents made for their children, so she assumed it was from her mother.

She stopped to switch off her computer, when her cat appeared. Her heart leaped into her throat.

'Fel, do you have to do that?' Hand on her chest, she breathed deeply until her calm returned.

The cat was a ghost, and telepathic as well as slightly psychopathic. *I'm bored*, it thought at her with a purr. It blinked its glowing, golden eyes.

'Do it on your own time. I'm heading out. Isn't there some other witch you can haunt today? I'm kind of busy.'

The cat licked its ghostly paws. The cat had been black with white-socked feet in life. Now, its body was a greyish shadow and its feet were transparent, so watching it lick non-existent paws was quite disconcerting. The sight of that long tongue licking air got her every time. She shuddered.

I need entertainment, Fel thought at her, blinking again. She looked pathetic. Then she massaged a pile of paper before settling herself down.

'Find a mouse and terrorise it. I'm heading out.'

The cat tucked its invisible paws under its greyish mass of chest. *A date?* Fel managed to express mild interest, in the way cats were interested in anything other than themselves.

'No, business.'

Looks like a date, Fel purred.

Elena shut the door, shaking her head. Silly cat, she thought with a smile.

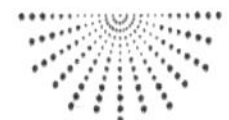

CHAPTER TWO

Jake Royston had arrived five minutes early on purpose—to assess his quarry, work on his angle, find her weaknesses and exploit them. Watching from a niche, where the pay telephones used to be, he waited. When she glided through the entrance, a frisson of electricity arrowed through his body. *What the hell was that?*

His gaze was riveted to her ginger hair, restrained in a clasp. He'd always been fascinated with that color. His fingers curled with desire to set the long strands free, to see them fall against the creamy skin of her neck. As she turned, seeking him, her bright, green eyes scanned the room. The smattering of freckles on an otherwise flawless, pale complexion, floored him.

Heart thudding, his gaze travelled hungrily over her body. He imagined running his hands over her full breasts and the soft curve of her hips. He licked his lips and willed his body to behave. This strong an attraction would be an impediment to doing good business.

Running his hand over his face, he tried to quell the rise of his blood. Looking back over to where she stood, waiting patiently, he realized he liked her face, too. Her intelligent eyes and solid brow only increased his interest. There was something about her, a quality he couldn't name, but only feel. He rocked back on his heels, smitten, just like that. Not possible, and yet… A smile crept over his features. The evening was going to be an amazing adventure. He knew it in his bones. He sent Pen a text, asking her to send his apologies to the Lowton's cocktail party. He had other plans for the evening.

I n the lobby, Elena waited. The foyer had a large clock, which showed that Mr Royston was seven minutes late. She shook her head. Damn him and his tactics. She had been exactly on time.

At least the restaurant wasn't too busy, not yet.

'Miss Denholm?' said a deep, rich voice behind her.

Elena swung around. 'Mr Royston?' Her gaze travelled from his feet to the top of his head. He was tanned, and well built, without being overly showy about it. He had startling blue eyes and nicely curved dark eyebrows. His mouth was generous and his smile, while not quite reaching his eyes, was dazzling.

If he were a warlock, he'd be in big trouble. He wore a charcoal-colored suit, bespoke, or maybe Armani. Either way, it was very fine. He exuded control, power and class.

'Yes,' he said with a nod, before offering his hand for her to shake.

Elena hadn't quite pulled herself together. He wasn't the crusty old man she'd been expecting. Thoroughly wishing that Gracie had warned her, she responded, putting her hand in his. Normally, she wouldn't have shaken his hand. It was a witch thing, avoiding the skin-to-skin contact, unless you wanted the intensity of it.

She gasped at the warmth of his skin. There was definitely an attraction there, and a sizzling amount of energy pouring out of him.

He narrowed his gaze. 'Is everything all right?'

'Yes, yes,' she said with obvious fluster. 'This is a lovely hotel, isn't it?'

He smiled at her, making her stomach do flip-flops. 'You like old buildings? This is one of my favorites.'

'Yes, I love them. I often go to the Queen Victoria Building, just to look at it.'

'Those Victorians knew how to build, didn't they? I come here a lot. Shall I show you around before we sit down?' Elena nodded. This was not what she'd been expecting.

The conference rooms were empty so Jake took her through them, pointing out the ceiling moldings, ornate cornices and the long narrow windows. 'I'd love to own an old house, but I don't think I ever will,' Elena said wistfully.

Jake looked at her and grinned. 'Me too. I live in an art deco period place. Not quite as old world as this, but it has character. There are a lot of old sandstone buildings in Bridge Street, near my office. I remember walking along that street as a teenager and not noticing how grand they were. Some even had statues in niches looking down. It's only now I notice them.'

Elena's gaze lingered on the moulded ceiling and chandeliers, and then Jake led her to another room. This one had been tastefully renovated, and included a large marble fireplace. She shivered once and sucked in a breath.

'Are you all right?' he asked.

'Yes, fine. Old buildings like this make we wonder what life was like in those days. I think about the spirits of those who died — whether they still linger.' She noticed his intense gaze and felt her face heat. 'Sorry, silly talk really.'

Jake grinned. 'Not at all. I'm not one for ghosts normally, but I can tell you, Port Arthur in Tasmania creeped me out.'

Grateful for his reassurance, she smiled. 'I've not been there myself, but I have heard the tales.'

They finished the tour of the conference rooms and headed back to the restaurant. Surprisingly, she was relaxed in Jake's company. She liked his informed description of the hotel building, and the way his eyes lit up when he talked. If only…

'Shall we go in? I reserved a table. Your assistant gave me the contact number,' she said when they were once again in the foyer. Standing aside, he held out his arm so she could precede him.

On entering the restaurant, she was having a hard time containing her nervousness. Looking at the rooms had been an ice breaker, and she had warmed to him in a way she hadn't expected. She was certain he liked her too, but now they had to get down to business.

Smoothly, he pulled out the chair for her, a courtesy she wasn't expecting. 'Thank you.' He really was catching her off guard. He took a seat opposite her and signaled for the waiter. She was trying to figure out if he was being polite, or dominating to win the negotiation.

The waiter came over. Jake turned to her. 'There's an excellent pinot noir served here. It's light and refreshing. Would you like to try it?'

A smile lit up his face and made his eyes sparkle.

His charm was working on her, but in the back of her mind she worried it was only a tactic.

'Yes, thank you.'

He ordered a Tasmanian Pinot Noir, and the waiter left to fill the order. Before Elena could launch in on the negotiations, Jake continued to talk about the history of the building, which had been a boutique hotel in Victorian times, and a barracks prior to that. If he was trying to help her relax it wasn't working. She wanted to keep the details of Grace's proposal in her head, but the sound of his voice chased it all away.

'Is something wrong?' he asked.

'No.'

'You qualified to represent Ms Riordon?'

She'd been leaning forward, and slammed back into her chair. 'In law? No, I'm Gracie's cousin. She asked me to negotiate for her.'

His smile faded, and there was a predatory gleam in his eye. 'Your cousin has been deliberately holding out to get top dollar. She's trying to screw my client for every cent.'

'You're wrong. She is against the development in principle. However, she is willing to sell if you agree to some terms.'

He leaned his elbows on the table, his gaze tracking over her face. 'She's in no position to discuss terms. She should take our overly generous offer and be done with it.'

'She is in a position. You may take her to court, but the judge won't be happy that you didn't negotiate, and I think the court would like her offer, too. It's very reasonable.' Her voice was calm and controlled. He was intimidating, but she wasn't going to back down, no matter how handsome his smile or how expert his small talk.

'I'm listening.' His voice was gruff and his expression neutral, except for his gaze. Those intense blue eyes never left her face.

Just then, the waiter appeared with the pinot noir in lovely, cut-crystal glasses. Elena couldn't help frowning at them. She'd been to restaurants a number of times, and had never been served in such special glasses. Her gaze flicked up to assess Jake Royston again. Was he some kind of top-notch client?

The waiter placed the wine carefully on the table. Elena was distracted by a commotion on the other side of the restaurant. Her gaze began to wander about the room. Something wasn't right. The vibe was wrong.

'You were saying,' Jake said as he picked up his glass.

Her gaze flicked back to him, and she returned to the topic. 'Grace is concerned about the environment. She is proposing that the development adopt the new voluntary standard for economically sustainable development with recycled water, solar energy and biodegradable sewerage and so on.'

He took a sip of his wine and lifted an eyebrow. 'I'm happy to put her proposal to my client, after a thorough analysis, of course. But really, she has left it rather late.'

'I'm sorry about that. Grace finds it…' Her attention was snagged by a fistfight, two people shoving at each other on the opposite side of the room.

'See someone you know?' he asked, and then took another tentative sip of the wine.

'No. Bad feeling, I expect. It happens sometimes. Looks like a fight or something.' She put her fingers on the stem of the glass and rolled it absently, while her mind was occupied.

Jake took another sip of wine and swallowed. 'A fight?' He turned in his chair to take a look before facing her again.

A savage stab of magic made her gasp and tip over her glass. Distracted by the red stain spreading over the white table cloth, Elena let out an unladylike screech. 'I'm sorry. I'm not normally so clumsy.' She cast her glance at Jake. He gazed into her face as if nothing had happened.

Righting the glass, she used her napkin to stem the flow of liquid. The wine had missed her dress, but not the blood red carpet. 'At least I didn't break the glass.' Her fingertips lingered on the delicate stem. Swinging around, she managed to get the attention of a waiter, who ran to fetch a cloth.

More noise distracted her. At the service door the altercation continued. It was a waiter, shoving people out of his way. There was something familiar about the back of the head. She gave a mental shrug. Backs of heads? What was she thinking?

Firm fingers encircled her wrist. With a squeak, she turned back to the table. Jake Royston, top lawyer and all round hot shot, had a hold of her hand. He had rather an intent look in his eyes.

'Mr Royston!' She tried to snatch her hand out of his grasp, but his grip was firm.

He stroked the skin of her wrist, a soft, gentle expression on his face. 'Call me, Jake. You're lovely. I think I'm in love.'

CHAPTER THREE

Elena's jaw dropped as she looked at her hand captured in his strong grip. Sweeping her surprise away, she let anger at his tactics take over, and her mouth firmed into a straight line.

She wiggled her fingers, but couldn't get loose. 'Mr Royston, about my cousin, Gracie's plot of land — ' She tried to extract her hand again, a quick snatch, but it didn't work.

A waiter arrived to clean up the spill so he had to let her go, though his blue gaze was intense and full of sexual promise. Elena's cheeks radiated heat. She licked her suddenly dry lips.

With both hands in her lap, Elena thought about what had happened. The stab of magic had definitely been a spell being let loose but she couldn't see where it had gone.

Jake Royston's tactics were putting her on edge. Her thoughts were in complete disarray, as were a number of hormones she had not experienced in a long time. Perhaps he was as attracted to her as she was to him, but to use flirtation to put her off guard was plain wrong.

'A fresh glass of wine, miss?'

'No, thank you. A water, please,' she said to the waiter. No wine for her, if he was going to play dirty.

The waiter, a tall, rangy, pimply lad, nodded, and efficiently cleaned up the spill. She had to remember to give him a good tip.

Jake lunged for her hand again, and she thrust it back into her lap. 'Really, Mr Royston. I know you're a top lawyer and all. I know I'm not. That doesn't make me stupid or gullible. My cousin has an excellent offer.'

She pulled the email out of her purse and slid it across table. 'I think you should consider it.'

She saw him watch her mouth, her lips. It was thoroughly disconcerting. 'Mr Royston? Are you listening to anything I'm saying?'

'I'm listening to every word. Do you know you have a dimple on one side of your mouth, and your teeth are perfectly shaped?'

She frowned at him. 'Really, Mr Royston. Could you please stick to the business at hand?'

'Of course.' He nodded absently, picked up the email and slid it into the inside pocket of his suit jacket. His gaze was centered on her mouth. 'Those full lips of yours are begging to be kissed.'

Elena rocked back in her chair. That magic couldn't have been directed at them, could it? 'Please tell me you're having a nervous breakdown or something?'

He frowned, tilting his head to one side, as if she'd said something odd. 'No, I feel fine, fantastic even.' A devastating smile lit his face and plucked at her heart strings.

Something was definitely wrong. *The magic spell?* She shook her head. It didn't make sense. Yes, there were witches and magic, but that didn't mean random people got zapped by spells for no reason.

He sat back, that smile lingering on the corners of his mouth. His eyes burned a path across her skin, which raised the heat levels in the room a few degrees.

'I feel great, actually.'

The vibe she was getting from him was intense. She knew he wanted to have her. Elena had to sit on her hands to stop from fanning herself. She looked around the room for some inspiration, trying to figure out how this business meeting had turned into a debacle.

'Please let me hold your hand. There's something I need to tell you.'

He reached out across the table and placed his hand in the middle, palm up. She stared at it for a few minutes, absently admiring the shape of his fingers. 'Why do you need my hand?'

'I want to hold it. Please?'

Looking from his outstretched hand to his face, she shook her head. 'That's intimate. We aren't intimate.'

She picked up her glass of water and gave him a small salute to stall for time. Her life had suddenly become complicated. She sent her senses out into the room, looking for the threads of the spell. It was definitely strong around them. She used her talent to feel around the edges, tracing the threads, following along the coils.

'Not yet,' he said, his voice low and rough as he withdrew his hand.

Elena's senses zeroed in on Jake. Shivers shot up her spine. A premonition. They were going to be intimate.

Again, he put his hand across the table cloth, palm up, and left it there. Grace was not going to believe that her negotiations had gone to hell and back. Giving a shrug and casting reserve to the wind, she placed her hand in his. His fingers latched onto her. He closed his eyes and breathed deeply. 'That feels wonderful. You're beautiful. Sexy.'

'I am?' She chewed her lip.

'I want to marry you,' he said, his voice dropping to a deeper level.

'What? No!' Her denial was instinctive. She wrenched her hand away to cover her mouth. It was then she smelt it — traces of magic from his hand. That spell *had* been aimed at them. But for what possible reason? What kind of spell?

Jake's face crumpled and he put his head in his hands, rubbing his brow. How low did she feel about hurting his feelings? She shook her head. It wasn't her fault, so she shouldn't feel bad for upsetting him. She reached out to sniff his wine — a touch of ginseng, a pinch of cinnamon and a heavy pall of magic. The stained portion of the table cloth was in front of her. She picked it up and inhaled. Her wine had been spelled, too.

A great whoosh of air came out of her when she sat back against the chair. She was flabbergasted. Someone had played a terrible joke. A love spell, on them? My, that would have been entertaining, to say the least. They probably wouldn't have made it out of the restaurant before copulating, given there was already some heady sexual attraction between them. She looked over her shoulder. It was a long way to the exit — definitely naked before reaching the lifts.

What a horrible thing to happen. Who could have done this? Them getting down and dirty would have created a sensation. The press would have had a field day, and what about poor Jake's reputation? At least she was a nobody to the general populace, but he was someone important, someone whose reputation was worth a lot.

She looked at Jake again, and his eyes were still locked on hers. She had a serious problem on her hands. With luck, the spell might weaken over time: a year, maybe two, but not anytime soon. Jake had been given a very strong dose, half a glass at least. He wasn't going to be functional. She couldn't let him go; actually, she doubted he would let her go.

A love spell affected the judgement. Jake made important decisions every moment of his working day. He could mistakenly agree to contracts, or give away his possessions. She had to stay with him, to make sure he didn't decide anything until she could get this spell removed.

The restaurant was starting to fill up with the dinner crowd. Things could get serious, and embarrassing. 'Jake, would you like to come home with me?'

Lifting his head, his eyes rounded and his smile swept away the misery of a few moments before. 'Yes, please.'

Elena nodded. 'Good. First, I want you to call your assistant. Have her cancel your appointments for the next few days. Tell her you're extraordinarily busy — don't wish to be disturbed, or something.'

'I like the sound of that.' He pulled out his phone and pressed the speed dial. He more or less said exactly what she had instructed, but there was a hint of the normal Jake there. His assistant's voice became shrill as he held the phone away from his ear.

'No, Pen. I'm fine. Just reschedule the lot of them. I don't care what excuses you make. I pay you to deal with that. No, I won't be contactable; my phone will be on silent.' He listened to her for a few more moments. 'No, I'm not going to reconsider. Tell the Stanton brothers that I said sign the deal or I'm walking. No, Pen, you deal with it. Yes, I'm currently with

Ms Denholm.' Jake's eyes had never left hers. Elena may have forgotten to breathe.

With a stab at the off button, Jake cut his assistant off mid-screech.

'Everything settled?' she asked.

'Yes. My assistant knows who pays her wages. Besides, she's good at what she does.' His smile was bright as he stood up, chucked some notes on the table and then took her hand again, guiding her out of the chair.

As she walked through the doorway, she wanted to fan herself. Jake Royston was a big hunk of man. Although the well-cut suit disguised the power underneath, he was braw and broad. What was she going to do? He wanted her, and that wasn't a half-bad proposition.

It had been a while since she'd indulged. The evil part of her mind reminded her that she had him at her mercy. However, there was no way she could take advantage of him. He wasn't in his right mind. It would be the worst kind of betrayal, sleeping with him when he had no choice in the matter. She'd have to do her best to keep him occupied and out of trouble until she figured out who had done this, and make them reverse it.

Outside in the peach light of dusk, he led her to his red, soft-top sports car, a BMW. The valet slid out of the car and tossed the keys to Jake. Elena hesitated. Was it even safe for him to drive?

He looked confident. It was only when he looked at her did he appear slightly deranged. Elena wanted to slap whoever it was who had cast the spell in the first place. She slid onto the leather seat, letting her gaze fall to his hand where it rested on the stick shift. He had beautiful hands, an artist's hands. She could imagine them on her skin. *Don't let your mind go there, girl. Big trouble. Understand? He's off limits.*

A sigh escaped her. 'Everything all right?' he asked, using that sexy, love-me voice.

'Yes, fine.'

'Where to exactly?' He lifted an eyebrow, a smile lurking at the corner of his mouth.

She gave him her address. Keeping him with her was the only way to contain this problem. She had to curtail his excursions and keep him occupied in her small two-bedroom semi-detached in Balmain.

Great. Keep him occupied and not take advantage of him sexually. How hard was that going to be? Well, she had moral fibre and a strong will, so she'd manage it.

First thing, she had to get Grace onto the problem. Surely her cousin and dearest friend had not set her up. As they sped along the onramp to take the Sydney Harbor Tunnel, she glanced at Jake's profile. A proud nose and an intelligent brow, too? Darn it. He was gorgeous. She turned away before he noticed her looking, her heart beating fast.

Keep your mind on the business at hand. Who could have done this? Who would have a motive? It would not surprise her if Aunt Elvira had cast the spell. She was always lamenting how Elena needed a good time in bed to set her to rights. Elena rolled her eyes upward. Elvira liked to have a man around, although she was discreet about it. Uncle Ernst had left before Elena had arrived on the scene. She remembered her aunt's voice. *We were a breeding pair, my dear. I don't mind. It was time for him to leave, and Grace gets what she needs from him.*

Elena would have to ask Elvira point blank whether she had hexed Jake, or at least ask Gracie to do it. Grace could face up to her mother better than Elena ever could.

In no time at all, Jake had taken the exit and was heading to Balmain. With a short cough of the brakes, Jake pulled up in front of her place.

'Cute. Flowers,' he commented, as he checked out the little garden at the front of the house, lit by her solar-powered paving lights.

She climbed out of the car and gulped. She was bringing a man to her home for the first time. Well, she was twenty seven, and it was about time, she supposed. 'Thank you. Come in.'

With a wide grin and a firm grip on her arm, he accompanied her along the path to the door.

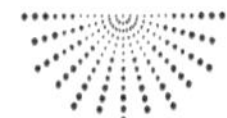

CHAPTER FOUR

Elena let Jake in. He stepped over the threshold, politely nodding as he looked around the room. Her living area had a three-seater sofa and two comfy chairs. As it was open plan, the kitchen area sat to one side, separated by a breakfast bar. A small dining nook was on the far side of the room. She locked the door behind her and dropped her keys on the desk by the door. 'Now, if you make yourself at home, I have to make a quick phone — '

Jake grabbed her, his mouth descending before she could finish her sentence. His mouth was hot, his lips firm and demanding. His tongue sought hers, and spears of lust enlivened her senses.

Her hands grabbed his lapels and she was lost. When she realized she was pulling him closer, she tried to squirm out of his embrace. With a hungry growl, he cupped the back of her head, deepening the thrust of his tongue. This man knew how to kiss. Her nipples ached and she was so wet and ready, she was in danger of ripping his coat off. Elena needed air. She put her hands on his shoulders, trying to fight the power of his kiss, which was wreaking havoc with her hormones.

Her fingers found shoulders, muscled and firm. Flashes of desire kicked through her as her hands travelled over his upper body and arms. Finally, her resolve solidified. This man was under a spell. *Back off*. She gave a firm push.

Jake released her mouth to bury his face in her neck. His warm breath excited her sensitive skin, the sensation even more intimate than the kiss.

Stifling a groan of desire, she stepped away from him. The room was way too warm, her breathing way too excited.

'We shouldn't do this.' She wiped the back of her hand across her mouth, tasting the spiced wine in a timely reminder of the spell.

'I thought you liked me.' His irises darkened.

'I do like you. We just can't kiss like that.'

He made to move toward her. She took a step back, coming up against the door.

'Why not? You seemed to like it. You taste divine. I want to kiss you…everywhere.'

A ripple of weakness left her breathless. His words conjured up images of him naked. Of her naked. Of them naked, together. 'You can't.'

He ran a finger along her cheek and brushed a thumb against her bottom lip. 'You want me.'

Elena closed her eyes. She couldn't deny it so she wouldn't try. 'We hardly know each other. I've got to make a phone call. Please, sit down. Make yourself comfortable. I'll be back in a minute. We'll talk then, okay?'

His gaze ate her up from the top of her head to the tip of her toes, making it hard to breathe. The warmth in her belly fueled the fire in her sex. It was the most sensual look she had ever received. He nodded and turned away, shaking out his shoulders before he sat on the sofa.

Elena thought her knees might buckle. She wasn't going to last against that. The blood throbbed at the juncture of her thighs. No teenage grope had left her so turned on.

'Why don't you make some coffee?' she said cheerily. 'I have a fab espresso machine. At least, I think it would be fab, if I could get it to work.'

Grace had given it to her, as she and Declan had received two for a joining present.

Jake's glaze flicked to the kitchen, and the gleaming chrome monstrosity sitting on the bench. There was a twinkle in his eye. 'Nice. How do you take it?'

The flash of his blue eyes reminded her how attracted she was. 'White and one, thanks.'

He moved off to the kitchen and squared his shoulders as he assessed the machine. Heading to her bedroom, she picked up the phone. Once inside, she leaned on the door so he couldn't come in after her and pressed the speed dial.

Grace picked up. 'Hi Elena. So how did it go? Have you ironed out that deal yet?'

'No, I haven't.' She kept her voice low.

'Why are you talking funny? Didn't he go for it?'

'We didn't quite get to the deal.' Elena lowered her voice further. 'Someone put a love spell on him. It was aimed at both of us, but I spilled the potion meant for me.'

'You're kidding me.'

'No, I'm deadly serious. He's besotted.'

Grace laughed, a full belly laugh. 'Excellent.'

'No, it's not excellent. I had to bring him here. He has it really bad.'

'Have you two…you know?'

'No, we haven't. I can't take advantage of him.'

'Why not?'

'It would be like raping him. He's not in his right mind. Did you set me up? Did you do this?'

Grace spluttered indignantly, 'No. I. Did. Not. Set. You. Up. But I wish I had. I've seen photos of him in the papers and celebrity magazines. He's gorgeous. He always seems to have some well-dressed and well-connected woman on his arm. Way to go, Elena.'

Elena shut her eyes. 'It's not funny—not good.' She pinched the bridge of her nose as she considered what Grace had told her. 'I believe you didn't do it. No one could be that excited by the prospect and have done it themselves. You have no guile in you. Your mother?'

Grace hummed to herself for a few seconds. 'It does seem like something Mama would do, but it wouldn't be like her not to tell me about it. A love spell with you and Royston has a serious gloat factor that my mother could not resist.'

'Can you ask her for me?'

'Of course, but you know she is with this new man of hers. She won't answer the phone. I think she's too far to hail. You might have to wait until she gets back.'

'When's that?'

'Let me see, new man, younger, virile. She older, horny as all hell. Could be three days before she surfaces, Monday, or late Sunday, if her partner's stamina fades.'

"But I thought she was working on the stall?'

'Darn, you're right. I forgot about that. That means it's just me. There goes my plans. Maybe you could mind the stall, bring lover boy.'

'Grace, no funning. We had a deal. The market only runs on Saturday.'

'I'm minding the stall. I get that part. So, what if it's not my mother?'

'Three days is a long time to wait if she didn't do it. Who else could it be, if it's not her?'

'I have no idea. I'll ask around. Love spells are specialized, particularly if it is as potent as you say. Someone must have bought ingredients, so that might narrow down the suspects.'

'Good thinking. Please, Grace, find out who did this. I may not make it through the next few days.'

'Is he as built as he looks in the society pages?'

'Uh-huh.'

Grace squealed. 'Lucky you!'

'I told you, I can't take advantage of him. I don't want to be up on charges of exploiting a human.'

'But you didn't cast the spell. You should relax and enjoy yourself.'

Elena shook her head and glared at the phone. Putting it back to her ear, she added, 'It's not real. He's affected by a spell. Without it, he might be attracted to me, but nothing more. We come from different worlds.'

Grace tut-tutted into the phone. 'Those human morals of yours mean a lot to you, don't they? Look, you're trying to make sure nothing happens. I understand where you are coming from. But if you slip up, can't hold out against all that man, then don't beat yourself up about it. You didn't put the spell on him. You're a victim here.'

Elena let out a slow breath and nodded. 'You're right. I am a victim. I like what you're saying, but I'm still no-touchie.'

'Right, then. I'll start making a few calls. Talk to you in the morning. Bye.'

As Elena ended the call, she leaned back against

the door and stared sightlessly at the ceiling. It was going to be a long night.

The aroma of fresh coffee filled her nostrils. 'Well, well, the man has a mechanical mind. That takes his score up to nine point five out of ten. Handsome, well-built and a handyman to boot.' Her sense of irony grew. *Great. Absolutely great. I'm supposed to resist all that.*

She flung open the door. On the kitchen counter were two steaming cups of coffee. Jake was stirring one of them. 'How on earth did you manage that? And don't tell me you read the instructions. So did I.'

He cocked his head to the side and handed her a cup. 'You haven't tried your coffee yet. The proof is in the tasting.'

She waved the cup under her nose and inhaled theatrically. That useless monstrosity had been sitting in her kitchen for a whole year, producing not so much as a drop of coffee. She lifted the cup and took a sip. Pure caffeine pleasure exploded in her mouth. 'This is great,' she said, taking another longer sip.

Jake smiled and her heart flip-flopped. That smile was rock star gorgeous and it caressed the very centre of her. Focussing her gaze on the coffee, she moved to the sofa as she drank some more. 'Take a seat and tell me the secret of the machine.'

He came and sat by her. 'It's probably easier to show you.' Her eyes crossed, and he laughed. 'Okay, it was the valve on the pipe connecting the machine to the plumbing. Once I opened it, the machine worked.'

'That simple?'

He nodded and drank his coffee, nursing the cup between sips in his palm. She gazed at his hands again, liking the symmetry of his fingers and the rounded cut of his nails. When she started thinking of his hands on her, she shot her gaze to the other side of the room. Maybe she had been affected by the love spell, after all. Her thoughts were unusually racy. It had been a long time since she'd had a man in her life. Actually, she'd barely been twenty. No wonder her coven family were keen to see her mated before her biological clock seized up.

Jake finished the last of his cup and put it on the coffee table. Half turning toward her, he began to play with her hair. Ignoring him was no deterrent. He unclipped her chignon and her hair fell around her shoulders.

'I love your hair. I wanted to do this the first moment I saw you.'

Her brows flew up. 'You did?'

That was before the spell. How odd. She loved the feel of his hands in her hair. His fingers crept along her head, and before long he was massaging her scalp. Eyes closed, she was practically purring.

Awareness returned. She gently disentangled her hair from his fingers, bringing it all over to the opposite shoulder. He took her withdrawal well, though she detected a certain amount of calculation in his expression.

'So, what should we do to pass the time?' she asked, thinking maybe they could watch a movie. Perhaps he was interested in watching the football. She hated football, but anything was better than sitting like this, trying not to touch each other.

His eyes glistened with a sexy gleam. 'Now that you mention it…' He moved closer.

Her eyes widened in alarm. His arm reached behind her on the couch, and he brought his body in front of her. 'You said we hardly know each other. Well, why don't we get to know each other better?'

His gaze traveled over her face, his fingers reaching up to touch her earlobe, sending another spear of excitement straight between her legs. She grabbed his hand, held it still and tried to breathe calmly. 'It would be lovely to get to know you better. Are you married, or with anyone?'

He shook his head, his gaze centered on her lips. 'You?' he asked in a low voice, which set off sentinels of alarm through her body.

'No,' she answered plainly. Perhaps she should've invented someone, some hindrance to being with him, but she hated to lie, even when telling the truth was goddamn awkward.

He moved closer. She inhaled the light scent of his aftershave. 'That is good news.'

His fingers began playing with her hair again, moving lower to stroke along her chin. His touch was electric. She sucked in a breath. 'Oh, goddess.'

There had to be a way to lessen the spell. From what she knew, it was nigh impossible to shift another person's spell, but maybe she could do something else to reduce the awkwardness, the longing.

'You like me touching you, don't you?' he asked, pitching his voice low and sexy.

Her eyes locked with his. He moved closer. His breath brushed against the skin of her neck, warm, moist, and pleasant. 'Yes,' she replied in a whisper.

Gently, his teeth nipped her earlobe and she shuddered, unable to dampen her reaction. She turned her head and he captured her mouth. One more kiss couldn't hurt, could it? His lips were silken. She opened to him, his tongue entering her mouth to duel with hers.

It was some hot kiss, Hotter than the one when they'd first arrived home. She wasn't fighting it, couldn't fight her reaction. He drew her closer. She clung to him, heart thumping in the back of her throat, making it hard to breathe.

He lessened the kiss, backing it off slowly. Without disengaging, he licked her bottom lip, sucking on it, caressing her face at the same time. It was more of a dance than a single act of kissing. He held her face in his hands and looked into her eyes. 'That was amazing…delicious.' He gave her a quick peck on the mouth.

She gaped at him stupidly. 'Yes…'

His arms surrounded her. She was leaning into him, her leg draped over one of his. How did she get like that? She was the one meant to be showing restraint. Leaning back, she lifted her leg, but he put his hand on her knee. 'Don't. Please leave it there. You feel good.'

'But we shouldn't be doing this. I shouldn't let you…'

His gaze flicked to hers, and there was desire there and something else — determination. 'You have no one else; I have no one else. There is nothing to stop us getting to know one another.' He ran his hand down the side of her face, from cheek to chin. 'You are very beautiful.'

'I am?'

'Yes,' he replied, dropping his voice so that it caressed her senses. 'I was pretty turned on, meeting you. I love how you look, how you move.'

Could that be the truth? That he thought she was hot before the hex? Elena narrowed her eyes as she examined his face, looking for a sign of insincerity. When she noticed he was studying her in return, it became difficult to breathe.

'So…tell me about you,' Elena said, needing a distraction despite enjoying sitting so near his heat.

Jake kept a close hold of her but leant his head back against the sofa and started to tell her about his life, boarding school, his parents' broken marriages and his focus on study and a career. He tried to keep his story matter-of-fact, but something on the edges, a quaver in his voice, hinted at more depth there. She discerned the lonely child, the betrayal of the parents, something she understood and that resonated within her. His focus she could understand. He was good at what he did, and had a successful career.

'You?' he asked, those intense blue eyes zeroed in on her.

Elena didn't talk about her history much. It wasn't like she could confess about her being a witch, or one of the folk. She talked about the things she liked, and her house and garden.

'There is something about you that makes me feel good.' He shook his head. 'Yes, that's it. You have a special quality, making others comfortable, warm, welcome.'

She turned to smile at him. His lips descended. She lifted her chin so their mouths joined. It was a light, playful kiss, and ended way too quickly. Still it was enough to get her blood racing. *Oh boy, I'm in serious trouble. Why does he have to be so kissable?*

'Thank you,' she said. 'Now, it's getting late. I think you should stay over.'

His eyes lit up, like lights on a Christmas tree. 'I'd love to.'

She climbed to her feet and he followed her. 'I have a spare room you can use.'

He stood stock-still. 'Spare room? But I want to be with you. I want to be in you.'

Elena looked up. A puppy love look was on his face. He was big and broad, and setting off all kinds of alarms in her system. 'I'm sorry, but we've just met. I wouldn't feel right taking it further so soon.'

Stepping clear, his hand rested on the small of her back. 'I hear what you're saying,' he said into her ear, brushing his lips against her neck. She shivered. This man had sex appeal. 'Just one more kiss to fuel my dreams?'

She ran her gaze over his face and centered on those luscious lips. Nothing harmful could come from kissing, could it? When he returned to his right mind he could forgive that, surely.

The puppy love look was melting her on the inside. He took her hesitation for a yes and seized her. She let out a squeak before his lips captured hers. The other kisses were hot: but this one consumed. He was no longer polite or restrained. This was a kiss to melt her, to set her on fire, to make her beg to be taken.

His hands traveled down and grasped her butt, lifting her up and pressing her against him. Oh God, what was that? His hard-on pressed against her. She prayed for mercy. Tonight was definitely going to be difficult. How was she going to resist all this man, when he wanted her so badly? Damn it all to hell, she wanted him too.

A kiss was all she could allow. Their mouths dueled and then broke apart. Jake nuzzled her neck, biting at the juncture, sending all kinds of pleasure spiking where it shouldn't. How was she going to stop this when all she wanted to do was surrender to it? She had to try to spell him; anything that would put an end to it.

She struggled out of his grasp. He lifted his eyebrow.

'I'm sorry. I can't do this,' she whispered desperately. 'You need to sleep now.'

She released the spell, and held him in it as he walked backward through the door. Gently, she pushed him onto the spare bed and let the sleeping spell keep him under. Tenderly, she brushed her fingers across his strong forehead and then slid her forefinger along his proud, straight nose. He looked peaceful in sleep, yet the strength still showed in the shape of his lips and the arrogant thrust of his chin.

She knelt down to undress him so he could sleep comfortably, hoping he wore underwear. His jacket came off easily, and so did his shirt. She hung these up in the closet. Turning back, she took in his sleeping form and the slow rise and fall of his chest, which had a smattering of dark hair in the center. He obviously worked out because he had impressively firm pecs, and he was rather stacked in his arms. Her gaze lingered for a bit, until she shook herself.

Next, she took off his shoes and socks, and considered the belt. His suit was Armani and she couldn't condone letting him sleep in his trousers. A spell was the best way to remove the belt. It was wrong for her to be groping around his midriff with her hands. Some would call it tempting fate. Still, she had to tug his trousers off, and that involved peeling the fabric from his hips and sliding it under his buttocks.

To her relief, he wore elegant-looking boxer shorts. His erection was still prominent. Her gaze centered on it. *I could have had that in me,* she lamented.

Hoping the sleep spell would merge with his natural sleep till morning, she put away the rest of his clothes. After draping a sheet over him, she switched off the light. *Damn that spell.* They might have actually liked each other without its interference. Once he came out of the spell he was going to be angry and vicious. With that chin of his, she could tell. He wasn't a top-notch lawyer for nothing.

CHAPTER FIVE

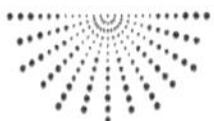

A sudden yell pierced Elena's pleasant dream. She bolted up in bed, panting. In the dark, she could see the digital clock displaying two a.m. A thump from the guest room told her Jake was awake. Luckily, she had planned for this contingency by wearing the ugliest nightgown she owned. It was made from scraps of old men's pajamas, haphazardly patched together. It was brown, cream and black, and very raggy.

'Rats,' she growled out as she threw off the covers. Darn her terrible spell casting. Being only half a witch had disadvantages. She had hoped he'd stay under till morning, but obviously her talent was too weak. She opened the door to the spare room and heard a cat screech as it ran out of the room. 'Fel, you rotten cat.'

The light was on. The cat bolted into the darkness. Jake stood there in his boxers, his hair up in spikes. 'It's a cat,' he said rather sheepishly. 'I'm sorry it startled me.'

Elena frowned. Fel had become a real, live cat, and she had no time to wonder at the how of it. 'I'm sorry. I didn't realise I'd locked her in with you. I'll go and put her out.'

She went to leave and his firm fingers tightened on her hand. 'Wait. The poor thing has had a bit of fright. Let it be for a while.' He looked down at himself. 'Did you undress me? I don't remember...' He shook his head, his pink cheeks betraying his embarrassment.

She grabbed the opportunity. 'Yes. You passed out. Sorry, I thought it best to put you to bed. Now the cat is out of the room maybe we can go back to sleep.' She yawned for effect.

'I'm not sleepy right now. Do you mind talking for a few minutes?' Her skin heated as his gaze passed over her body. Obviously, the ugly nightie was not as off-putting as she'd hoped.

'Sure,' she said, feeling quite the opposite as she stepped further into the room. This close to his naked upper torso, all her nerve endings tingled. He certainly exuded confidence, energy and sex appeal. Clenching her hands by her sides helped her to avoid reaching out to touch the smooth skin of his shoulders. Her gaze lingered on him; he was made so beautifully.

He smiled at her. Had he noticed that she couldn't keep her eyes off him? She hoped not. He pointed at the chin-up bar. 'So what's with the equipment? You work out?'

She gave a little laugh. 'No, I use it for my craft. I make items to sell at the market. I hang them from there while I work.'

His eyes lowered, lessening the heat. 'Can you do chin-ups?'

She drew her head back, surprised by the question. 'I don't think I've ever tried.'

'I'll show you. Come on.' He moved over to the chin-up bar, looking up at it.

'What? It's two in the morning.' *Oh lord. He's wearing boxers and he's so buff.* She tried looking away from all that flesh, not quite believing the predicament she was in.

'Come on, it won't hurt. I'll show you. Then you try.'

Elena ran her hands through her hair, straightening out some tangles. She supposed it was reasonable — bizarre, but reasonable. If he was doing chin-ups, he wouldn't be seducing her, would he? Perhaps the exercise would tire him out.

'Go ahead.'

She sat on the bed and watched him leap up to grab the bar. He managed it smoothly and then lifted himself up and put his chin above the bar, and then lowered. Elena's eyes bugged out. He had a six-pack, and all of the muscles on his chest and arms bunched under his skin, giving her an impressive display. She coughed when she thought about his body on hers. It was hard to not to begin fanning herself.

He did about twenty repetitions and then let himself drop. 'Your turn.'

'Me? I don't think I could do what you did.'

'Try it. Come on, I'll lift you up.'

Reluctantly, she walked over to the bar. She usually used a ladder or magic to tie her charms to the top. It looked far away. His hands gathered around her small waist and lifted. She reached up to grasp the bar and, when she had a grip, he let go.

'Now pull yourself up.'

He stood casually with his arms folded, but there was calculation in his gaze. With complete concentration, she tried to pull herself up, but lacked the upper body strength to do so. After a few lackluster tries, she dangled there, her arm muscles burning. 'I can't. Can you help me down?'

'Certainly,' Jake replied, enthusiastically.

He stood in front of her and slid his hands up her legs, underneath her nightie.

'What are you doing? Get me down.'

He hooked his fingers into the elastic of her underpants, drew them down her legs and flung them on the floor. 'I will. But I'm doing it my way.'

While Elena dangled from the chin-up bar, Jake ran his hands up her legs and grabbed her buttocks in both hands, supporting her so she wouldn't fall. He put his head under her ugly nightie and his hot breath scorched the flesh of her inner thighs.

'You mustn't do this, Jake.'

She was shaking, from excitement, and from holding onto the bar. Her muscles protested. She would have to let go soon. Then she realized where his head was. *He wasn't going to do that, was he?*

His tongue ran up the skin of her left inner thigh. Her eyes rolled up. *He was going to do that.* He ran his firm, hot tongue up her right thigh. She nearly lost her grip.

She dropped a little lower and his tongue delved between her labia. Holding her by her butt, he delved deeper, seeking her clitoris. He was an expert with his tongue and teased her, making her open to him, seeking the core of her pleasure.

Elena stared to groan as tendrils of heat snaked through her, over and over again. He used his shoulders to wedge her legs open, exposing her vulnerability and taking her weight. He concentrated on her clitoris, gently sucking and then expertly flicking it with his tongue. The orgasm was building. She couldn't fight it. It was all she could do to hang on as she started to scream and buck against his hold.

Not able to hold on any longer, she let go. He lowered her down, easing her legs off his shoulders so that she slid down his body. He stripped the nightie from her so that their naked flesh could glide together. With her heightened sense of touch after her orgasm, the heat of his skin was intense. As her sex neared his, she realized he was naked and ready. Distracted by hanging onto the bar, she hadn't noticed him slipping off his boxer shorts. Just when had he put that condom on? Cunning, he was. Downright cunning.

She tried to stop her glide by pushing her hands against his shoulders, but his strength won out. His lips snagged hers in a potent kiss. It served to distract her as he continued to lower her down onto his erection. The tip nudged between her moist labia.

Breaking the kiss, she tried to reason with him. 'Jake, please. Don't do something you'll regret.'

'I won't regret this. I've been dying to have you since I first laid eyes on you.' And then he entered her with a swift thrust of his hips. He filled her up.

'You're so wet. Succulent,' he groaned into her ear. She clung to him, not believing how hard he was and how great it was to have him inside her. It had been so long since she'd had any action.

He shifted her in his grip, urging her legs around him. He held her by the hips and began to move.

The pressure built as he thrust inside her — he had so much control and experience. Jake knew how to pleasure a woman. She was in serious trouble. This was a lover who could make a woman weep, and break her heart as easily as he'd seduced her. Didn't Grace say he always had some woman hanging off him? No wonder. She couldn't be one of them. When this spell ended, he wouldn't be interested. She had to remember that.

'Kiss me,' he demanded, and she responded. There was no fighting him, his appeal, his downright sexual dominance.

Their lips met. His hunger for her made him wild as his lips sought hers. She held on as his pace increased. He took a few careful steps with her in his arms and rested her back against the wall. This gave him more leverage to delve deeper into her. Elena held on, his shoulder muscles bunched, his skin smooth under her fingers. She let herself go. She could fight the building orgasm no longer.

'Come,' she said. 'Please.'

'Not yet.' His words were harsh in her ear. Still her body reacted, pieces of her starting to float away. He was working her, knowing how to ride her for maximum effect. She tried stifling her moans of pleasure, but then he'd thrust and hold and then thrust again, breaking down all her defenses.

The noise she made sounded almost inhuman. An incoherent expression of lust bubbled out of her mouth.

Suddenly, he changed positions again. This time he placed her on the bed while she clung exhausted to his shoulders. Kneeling down, he grabbed her to him by sliding her along the mattress. It was an amazing feeling — vulnerable, possessed and dominated, and yet exhilarated.

He lunged inside her. Her vaginal muscles contracted, sending her already heightened pleasure centre into a spin. She couldn't believe he'd upped the pace again. She was so wet, his cock sliding into her created an amazing friction. He fit so well inside of her. Rational thoughts about how this wasn't real, and wasn't meant to be, skittered away. She was in the moment, meeting his thrusts, angling her hips even when he rotated his to excite every part of her.

The sound of her pleasure filled her ears. She wasn't even embarrassed by the noise she was making. He grunted and growled, and the sounds he made sent her higher. He was undoing her, sending parts of her in different directions.

He began to tremble. She sensed he was close, that his control was crumbling. She let herself go with him. Three more thrusts and he shuddered, letting out a roar. His orgasm came over him. He was vulnerable at that moment. She cherished the transformation in his expression. Then he lowered himself, face between her breasts, arms by her side.

For a few moments, they lay there and breathed together.

With his chin resting between her breasts, he gazed at her. 'You see? Now we know each other better.'

Elena had to laugh and let a chuckle rise from her gut. He levered himself up and lay down beside her. 'You didn't enjoy it?' he asked, dark brows furrowed together. A gentle finger on her chin urged her face in his direction.

Her chuckle became a full belly laugh. His mouth drew into a thin line. Calming, she reached up and stroked his face. 'That was amazing.'

He relaxed his expression and smiled, a satisfied 'I'm full of prowess' smile. 'Good.'

Next he was sliding his arms under her.

'What are you doing?'

'Putting you to bed.'

After kicking the door open, he carried her into her room. She caught sight of the cat, perched in the middle of the living room, illuminated by a shaft of light.

Satisfied? she thought at her.

Fel lifted a paw and licked it diligently. The paw

was white, furry and real. How had the cat done it? *Clever tom*, Fel thought. Then the cat settled on the carpet with what appeared to be a smirk.

Jake moving her to the bed cut off her line of sight, and then he kicked the door shut and everything went dark.

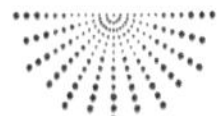

The digital clock showed 3.30 a.m. Jake slept beside her, his arms curled around her middle. That encounter had been an amazing experience. One could easily get addicted to it, to Jake.

Despite his alluring energy, she had to remember they were from different worlds. It was an accident. Not to be repeated.

Even knowing that, she desired his touch as if he had woken a part of her that had been lying dormant all her life. How happy she was to discover she had a sensual side. Now that she understood that, she couldn't deny it.

Perhaps she would have to date Drew, the grumpy warlock, after all, and give him a chance. He might be a jerk, but maybe he was good in bed. What choice did she have? It would break Elvira's heart if she ran off with a human and further weakened the coven. That would make her as bad as her mother.

It was difficult to sleep with Jake beside her. She'd never slept with a man in her bed before. How could she relax with him touching her, his small twitches and movements, and the sound of his breathing? She lay there watching the clock, anticipating no sleep and secretly enjoying the feel of his body against hers.

Sleep must have claimed her, because she was waking up with the most stimulating sensations running through her. Her breasts were being caressed, while one nipple was being deliciously suckled. Her back arched, giving Jake greater access. He switched nipples and his hand slid between her moist folds. Already, she was slick with arousal. How did that happen? She'd been asleep.

He worked over her breast, drawing her nipple deep until it hurt, giving both pleasure and pain. He moved up her body and caught her gasp between his lips, sending his tongue to meet her own.

How did this start again? It was not meant to happen.

His fingers slid inside. Her whole body bucked as he probed her depths, seeking to give pleasure as he dragged kiss after kiss from her. *This guy was an expert*, she thought. Her sex throbbed.

If her thoughts weren't in disarray she could have spelled him, just enough to allow her to escape from the bed. However, he kept her occupied, attacking her erogenous zones with practiced flair. He kissed down the column of her throat and then bit her gently at the juncture of her neck. Her back arched off the bed and then he was on top of her.

'Ready?' he asked, his voice hoarse with passion.

'Oh, goddess,' was all she could get out before he nudged her legs apart and speared her. Her body was so sensitized, she almost came as his heavy erection pierced her sex. A few lunges and she was making that noise again, the incoherent cries and groans of pleasure. These seemed to egg him on. His rhythm increased.

He stopped, and, keeping himself inside her, he lifted her hips as he adjusted his position, bringing his knees further up the bed so that he had to lift her to thrust. She was putty, like something he could re-form at will.

The thrusting started again, only more vigorous, and faster. His hands on her hips sent all kind of flutters into her belly. He was so dominant, lifting her easily and impaling her with his impressive cock. Her pleasure was intense. She reached up and held onto the bedhead as he plunged into her, their flesh meeting with satisfying ease. Her eyes closed as she lost herself in the rhythm of their joining.

Suddenly, he stopped. Her eyes flew open. There was a smirk on his face. She lifted her head and met his heated gaze. He disengaged, moving further down the bed. As he dragged her down to align her hips to his face, her soul surrendered.

'You're delicious,' he said as he put his hot mouth on her. Her body jerked as his tongue teased, sliding silkily between her engorged labia. How powerful was the sensation of his tongue running over that sensitized flesh? A deep, gut-wrenching groan escaped from her throat when he latched onto her clitoris and suckled gently. An orgasm overtook her in moments, waves of ecstasy swamping her again and again.

Next, he was plunging inside of her before the orgasm faded, drawing her up a rung or two of pleasure. She grabbed onto him, wanting to touch him, wanting the exquisite feel of his firm flesh beneath her hands. He radiated heat, and lust, and joy. In this moment of contact, she could feel those deep emotions from him. He was honestly and truly enjoying fucking her.

Taking the initiative, she drew herself up and kissed him savagely. That emotional connection could not be denied. He may be spelled, but he was enjoying her at the most basic level. Later, there might be recriminations, but right then, they didn't come into it. She ended up on his lap. They both brought abdominal muscles into play as they immersed themselves in a sensual dance. He held her as she arched her back, surrendering to her orgasm. With a few well-timed jerks of his hips, he came too.

He fell onto the mattress, bringing her with him. 'God,' he said. 'Oh, God.'

Elena's mind floated somewhere out of reach. 'Mmm?' was all the response she could muster.

'That was intense — so intense.'

'It was...'

Looking down the length of his body, she noticed he'd been wearing a condom. 'Where did you get that from?' She didn't have a supply. She passed him a tissue so he could dispose of it.

'I have a pocket in my boxers, just the right size for a little stockpile.'

Her brow furrowed. 'Why?'

He grinned. 'You never know when you are going to have the opportunity.'

She frowned and looked at him sideways. 'I see. So, you have sex with a lot of women?' It made sense. He was good at it, and had a hot body, along with a certain amount of charm.

'It's not politically correct to talk about the women you've had to the woman you're with. Besides, they meant nothing to me.' He grabbed her to him. 'You, on the other hand, mean everything.' He gazed at her at length, until she lowered her lashes. How could she bear that look, knowing it was a spell? She had to stop this right now. Maybe he would sue her for gross embarrassment when the spell was removed.

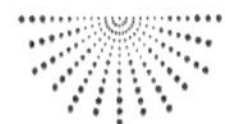

CHAPTER SEVEN

Elena must have dozed off because she woke to the sound of someone knocking on the front door. The bed was empty. She blinked away confusion and sleep.

The sound of the shower running reached her. She wrapped a sheet around herself and went to see who had come calling. Grace's pregnant silhouette showed through the frosted glass. A quick glance at the microwave display, and she frowned. Surely the markets weren't over yet.

Opening the door with a spell, she met Gracie's smirk as she came in. 'No need to ask what you've been doing. You look well and truly ravished.'

Elena straightened up. 'Very funny. What are you doing here? I thought you were tending my stall.'

Gracie slowly lowered herself down on the sofa, groped around in her purse and held up a wad of money. 'I did, and you sold out about an hour ago. Those Rozelle markets are really good. I bought heaps of things for myself. Out of your takings, of course.'

'Sold out. You're sure?'

'Yes. I have orders for fifteen more. I wrote them in your book.'

Elena plonked herself down next to Gracie. 'That's not happened before.' She pushed her tangled hair out of her face and eyed the cash. Her stall was really taking off.

'A lot of people said they'd heard about your good health charms and came to the markets especially. One guy had come out on the early morning train from the Blue Mountains. I was impressed, even though he was a little weird. He said they had real magic in them.'

'That's good, I suppose. Good that people are buying them. Not good that someone is saying out loud they have real magic in them.' Grace dropped the money in her lap — over $2000. Elena picked up the cash and stared at it.

Jake walked into the room, wearing his Armani trousers and nothing else. Grace took him in from head to toe, her eyes lighting up. She levered herself up from the couch and put out her hand. 'Hello, I'm Grace Riordon.'

'Riordon? Ah yes, the development.' Jake had a big smile on his face, like he had got all the cream. He took her hand and shook it decisively.

Elena stood up, and Jake dropped Grace's hand. 'We can't talk about the negotiation now.' She gave Grace a warning look, which she ignored.

'So, did Elena tell you about my proposal?'

Jake looked wide-eyed and innocent. He had barely listened to her when the spell hit. Elena found herself gritting her teeth. It was plain wrong to talk to him, wrong, like her sleeping with him. *Oh, goddess help me*, she thought, staring at the ceiling.

'A little…we became occupied by other things. Although, I will turn my mind to it shortly.' He sat on the couch but his eyes never strayed from Elena's face. They were like hot coals, searing a path to arousal. Elena tried to break eye contact. It was ridiculous. She wasn't affected by the spell, so why was she reacting like this?

Grace looked like she was about to say more until Elena threw up her hands. 'No, don't go there. Look, I'm hungry and in funds. Let's go up to Balmain Road and have brunch.'

Grace pouted. 'I'm sorry. I can't. I have an errand to run for you, remember?'

'But Grace, this is important.' Elena looked meaningfully at her and waggled her eyebrows. 'You can entertain Jake while I have a shower.'

Grace grinned at Jake and gave a little shake of her shoulders.

'I can keep you company in the shower,' Jake said. Elena caught his look, his eyes, dark with lust. She shuddered, as if he had stroked her clitoris. *What is wrong with me? I've never been in lust this bad before.* Maybe a cold shower would work, and a little more determination. She couldn't sleep with him again.

Grace came to her rescue. 'Okay, I'll stay a bit longer. Keep Jake company.'

Fel jumped up on the sofa. Grace's mouth dropped open and then clicked shut. 'Is that Fel?'

The cat meowed and did a convincing job of pretending to be a real cat by rubbing itself against her hand. Grace narrowed her eyes as Fel purred loudly.

'Don't ask.'

Grace leaned in closer to the cat. 'How odd. What on earth are you doing, Fel?'

The cat meowed again, then curled up on the arm of the sofa and went to sleep. Grace blinked a few times as the cat thought something at her. Elena couldn't catch it. Fel's barbs were always one on one.

Jake glanced at the cat with a smirk on his face. Fel had given him a lucky break.

After frowning at the cat a bit longer, Grace tossed her dark hair over her shoulder.

'Any chance someone could make a coffee?'

Jake shot up off the sofa. 'Yes, wait there. You, Elena?' The way he said her name made her melt on the inside.

'No, I'm fine. Shower.' She jerked a thumb over her shoulder to indicate where she was going. She backed out of the room, praying that nothing would go wrong. Grace was a much better witch than she was; maybe she could learn something about Jake's condition and the spell while Elena showered.

It was a warmish day. Elena turned the hot down low and had an almost cold shower. Washing herself only reminded her of their lovemaking — no, sex. There had to be emotion involved to use the word love. Jake may think he was in love but he knew women, and he knew how to the play them. She had to remember he was going to wake up, recover from the spell, and be bitter about wasting his time with her.

The big question was whether she was going to regret the encounter.

CHAPTER EIGHT

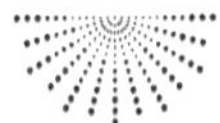

Mild sunlight bathed them as they sat on the street side of the De Fleur cafe, one of Balmain's better eateries, watching other locals do their shopping or drink coffee. Normally Elena would find it relaxing, but every time she looked across the table at Jake, he was gazing at her intently, making her sex throb.

Grace had decided that she was famished and joined them for brunch, although she had made a couple of calls in the backyard while Elena dressed in a pink sundress and strappy sandals.

Picking up her cup, Elena took another sip of her café latte. When she put it down, Jake reached for her hand again, rubbing his thumb along hers and sending all kinds of sparks through her skin. Given she was so affected by his touch, she again considered the possibility she had been spelled after all. Surely all this lust wasn't coming from her.

'Jake, could you excuse Grace and me for a moment?' She stood up, and jerked her head in the direction of the toilets. Grace, seeing her intention, stood and grabbed her purse before following.

'Won't be long,' Grace said to Jake, flashing him a

broad grin. Elena could tell that her cousin liked Jake, and appreciated his physique.

Elena pushed through the doors to the ladies and whirled around.

'What is it?' Grace asked, rubbing the top of her baby mound.

'Grace, am I under a spell too?'

Grace placed some of her dark shoulder length hair behind her left ear, and closed her eyes. The light touch of Grace's magic flowed over her. Elena gasped when Grace probed deeper. 'You don't appear to be affected. You seem quite happy. Why do you ask? All that hot-blooded man boiling your blood?'

Elena turned away and checked her face in the mirror. 'You could say that. I tried to keep it platonic, but he outmaneuvered me. Now all he has to do is look at me and I'm ready to jump him.'

Grace leaned back against one of the washbasins. 'I remember what that was like. Declan was particularly devious in gaining my attention. Once we grew up, I mean. He had to work hard for me to take him seriously, but when I noticed him...' She fanned her face, her expression one of contentment.

Elena sighed. She had witnessed the emotion, the lust, and ultimately the love that bound her cousin to her mate. 'That's all right for you. Declan is a warlock, and, hence, acceptable. Jake is not acceptable.' She closed her eyes and pushed down the emotions she was feeling. There was no future. He was a womanizer, and a human. As soon as the spell was lifted, he'd see her with different eyes. He'd be angry and hurt. She hadn't done right by him, but she was at a loss to know how she could have done better. An expert at working her defenses, it was if, around him, she didn't have any. Putting on a bright smile, she said, 'Now, any leads for me on those ingredients?'

Gracie gasped. 'I forgot. I have a list of names.' She pulled out a scrap of paper and ran her forefinger along the list as she showed it to Elena. 'These seven people recently bought three of the ingredients commonly used in love spells.'

Grabbing the list, Elena ran her eyes down it. Mary Jo Kemp, a 65-year-old witch, who wouldn't hurt a fly, and Geoff Sanders, a middling warlock, but one she didn't know well. There didn't appear to be any strong connection between them. The other names meant nothing until she reached the last one. 'Rory Penderton?'

'Drew's father,' Grace replied, nodding, her dark eyes serious. 'He lives out Homebush way.'

Elena lifted her head and stared into the middle distance. 'I've not met him.' Her gaze shifted back to Grace. 'But that's too close a connection, don't you think? Drew's father. Me, love spell?'

Grace shrugged. 'What would it gain him to spell someone other than his son? I can understand if the date had been with Drew...not very fair, mind you.'

Elena finger combed her hair. 'Let me see, there are stacks of motivations: humiliation, or revenge for spurning his son's advances.'

Grace stared at the ceiling for a few minutes, rolling her tongue inside her mouth. 'That is possible, I suppose. I don't know Penderton well at all. Mother doesn't like him much. Something about the past...'

'We better join Jake before he runs off.'

Grace chuckled. 'That's not likely is it? Not the way he eats you with his eyes.'

Elena paused, remembering how he'd gawked at her over her coffee. If only that look was real...and possible.

'Look, I'll try Penderton, can you check these other two? Harris and Beckford? I don't know them either. If we have no luck, we'll try the others, as un-likely as it seems at this moment.'

'Sure. I have time before Declan comes home. Still no word from mother.'

Elena repressed a sigh. Typical. Elvira was slippery at the best of times, and when you needed her was her best time to be absent. Her aunt called it character building when they were growing up. Problems that needed solving were their own responsibility. Rarely did she have to intervene once Grace and Elena had sorted something out.

When they returned to the table, Jake was on the phone, talking business. Elena panicked. She couldn't have him negotiating a deal while under the influence. What could she do though?

'Yes, I'd appreciate it,' Jake said into the phone.

She reached out and touched his hair. He paused, turned slightly, and smiled. It was dazzling. The voice on the phone was still talking. 'I'll remember the favor come bonus time. Thanks. Drop them off to the address I told you. Bye, and thanks.'

He ended the call. Elena lifted a curious eyebrow. 'Everything all right with you?' she asked carefully.

He stood up and stroked her face, bringing his forehead to rest against hers. 'It is now.'

A shiver passed through her, sending a jolt through her sex. She stepped away from her seat, her labia engorged and throbbing. Swallowing, she managed to say, 'Grace is heading off now.'

Smiling, he held out his hand. 'It was lovely to meet you, Grace.'

Her cousin held out her hand and sent Elena that look. The look that said 'Goddess! He's gorgeous and have a great time.' Elena returned the smile weakly. The day was going to be exquisite torture.

After they waved Grace off, she turned to him. 'I

have an errand to run out to Homebush. Would you like to join me?'

'Sure, I'll drive us out there. It's time I gave my car a decent run. Short city trips do it no good at all.'

'Ready?' she asked, as he drank the last of his second espresso. She swirled her hair into a bun and clipped it for the journey.

He nodded decisively and helped her from her chair. Elena paid the bill before they headed back to her place and Jake's car.

The spell didn't seem to affect Jake's ability to drive. He was wily and skilled, negotiating the traffic through to Victoria Road. He had the top down and wisps of hair escaped from her bun. She clawed the strands from her face and tried to see how close they were on Jake's GPS. Jake took another turn and cast a glance her way.

'Are you okay? You look worried.'

She flashed him a smile. 'I'm fine, just thinking.'

Thinking, thinking, like what was she going to say to Rory Penderton. She'd never met him. Now she was going to rock on in, and accuse him of hexing a complete stranger and trying to hex her. After having met Drew, she wasn't keen on meeting the father.

She hadn't bothered to hail or call beforehand. Rory would feel her approach because he was bound to have wards around the house.

The older folk tended to do that, establish wards. Elena only had them set when she went away, or if she was particularly afraid at night. Grace usually set them for her, because they were beyond Elena's talent. Once she'd inadvertently thrown an intruder through a window and part of a wall. Although Aunt Elvira was impressed with the hint of great talent the strength of her defense had shown, Elena had not ever repeated it. A ward was less intimidating, and didn't need explaining to the police. It put humans off without them knowing. It was no shame to her to get her talented cousin to set one when she needed it.

They pulled into the driveway of an old weatherboard cottage, painted grey with white trim. It had a stained glass panel on the front door. The house and garden were reasonably neat, but not very big.

She sat in the car for a bit, feeling about with her senses, testing for wards. There was a ward, a mild repelling spell to keep out the ordinary passer-by. She sent a hail into the house. *Rory Penderton. I'm Elena Denholm, may I come in?*

Warmth spread on the back of her neck. Jake had put his hand there. 'Are you okay?'

'Yes,' she whispered. He was very close. Next thing she knew, he was kissing her. She opened to him. His kiss wrote domination all over her. He controlled it, letting out enough passion to swamp her and dampening it down when she tried to ease off. He drew her closer and she brought her hands up to his chest, hoping to push him away, but then his strength and the firm muscle and the heat of him caressed her palms. She wasn't fighting anymore; she was clinging to him, until she was a warm, languid thing in his arms.

Backing off, his eyes were dark with passion. Elena could only gape at him, stupidly. What was that? How did he make her feel that way?

Part of her was scared. She didn't want her heart broken, but already knew it was a work in progress. She stroked his chin, rubbed her thumb across his lower lip. 'Jake, what are you doing to me?'

'Loving you,' he replied, his eyes twinkling with humor. He had a satisfied look on his face.

'Look, we'll have to talk about that. There is something I need to explain.' She wasn't sure how to broach the subject of the love spell, but she had time to think of something.

'Tell me.'

'Later. Right now I have to talk to someone inside. I won't be long. Do you mind waiting here in the car for me?'

There was a slight lowering of his eyelashes. 'Yes, sure.' He wasn't happy about it, she could tell.

'I…look, I don't know this person, so I don't feel right inviting you in. Give me a chance to get the lay of the land. I'll come and get you after that.'

His eyes widened. 'Sure. No problem. Are you sure you're okay? You seem nervous.'

'I'll be fine.' She slid out of the car and headed up the drive. She walked through Penderton's ward like a knife through soft butter. She began to think Penderton was even less skilled than she was.

He hadn't answered her hail, but he was home and waiting. He couldn't hide that from her. The front door was ajar so she pushed it open, alert to traps. 'Hello, may I enter?'

A shadowy figure rushed at her. She deflected the spell, ripped it to grey rags. Rather amateurish and half-hearted, she thought, although it would have been enough to scare an ordinary human. She needed to reserve judgement until she met the man. It was only fair.

The hall divided the house leading straight to the back. All of the adjoining rooms had their doors shut. That was okay, because she could feel Penderton was at the rear of the house, waiting. She walked along the dark corridor, her sandals clunking on the polished floorboards. The light was dim in the hall, but the crimson glass inset on the door let in a rose-colored glow.

The house had a nice vibration to it, despite Penderton's attempts to scare her off. Or maybe not scare her off, in particular, but people.

At her touch, the door swung open. She blinked at the sudden flood of sunshine. It was a veranda, enclosed by windows. Sitting at a small table, with a little red teapot that had steam curling out of its spout, was Rory Penderton.

He stood as she entered. About five foot ten, he was greying above the ears, and he was quite stocky. She thought he was about fifty, but you could never tell with warlocks because they aged more slowly than normal humans. His skin tone was olive, like Drew's, but his eyes were a clear grey, not dark like his son's. He had regular features, and was rather good looking for an older man.

Rory Penderton stood there and stared at her with his mouth slightly agape.

'I'm Elena. I'm sorry for troubling you, but something important has happened. I need…need to ask you about it.'

He seemed to shudder once before springing into action. 'Forgive me, please, take a seat. Tea?'

Elena relaxed at his tone. His voice was pitched at a level to soothe her anxiety. 'Yes, thank you,' she said as she sat down. Her gaze caught sight of a lovely garden through the windows. She could see that he spent a lot of time growing things, and growing them beautifully.

'What a lovely garden,' she said, with a smile. There was a flowering jacaranda tree in the corner, and a beautiful frangipani. One day she'd like a garden big enough for those types of trees.

Penderton's eyes tracked over her face down to her hands. 'What is it?'

'You're Pris's daughter aren't you?'

'Yes. You knew my mother?' Elena swallowed. Pris was a taboo topic, with Elvira, at least.

He nodded, his eyes taking on a glazed expression as if he was looking back in time.

'We were once close, she and I.'

Elena was puzzled and disturbed. He'd known her mother well, if his reaction was anything to go by. Why hadn't Elvira said? She would have liked to have spoken to someone who had known her mother during those years when she was getting to know that she was a witch, and part of a coven. She couldn't remember her mother, and no one knew where she was, or if she was even alive.

'So what brings you out here to see me today? Looking for Drew?' He grinned knowingly.

Elena picked up the tea and took a sip. It was Earl Grey; not a favorite. 'I'm not sure I'm looking for Drew. You see, someone cast a spell, a love spell. I'm afraid it caught a human.'

Rory Penderton's eyes widened. 'Why would you be coming to see me about that?'

She put her cup back in the saucer and used the handle to turn it back and forward as she thought about how to proceed.

'Three essential ingredients for a love potion were purchased in your name.' Elena decided she may as well go for it. 'I've come to ask you to remove the spell. I won't make a complaint about this. The human, though, may have other ideas.'

He sat back in his chair and lifted his hands in a helpless gesture. 'But I didn't buy any ingredients. I haven't practiced the craft of potion making for quite a while. My heart isn't in it.'

Elena believed what he said. There was something heartfelt and sad in his words. 'So, do you know who would have bought those ingredients under your name?' Elena had a pretty good idea.

Rory Penderton shrugged. 'No, I don't.'

'Surely your son?'

His expression became flushed with anger. 'Leave him out of this. Everyone is so quick to judge him. Isn't it enough that you spurned him, humiliated him?'

Elena stood up, her fists clenching. 'Look, I don't know what Drew told you. But we went on a date and it didn't work out. We didn't gel. There was no spurning, humiliating or anything remotely like that. It just didn't work.'

He sat still, his breathing calm. 'Oh. But I – '

She leaned back in her chair, feeling sheepish. 'Don't worry. I can guess. Drew is kind of surly, so I can well imagine what he said. Do you know where he is?'

Penderton shook his head, then got out of his seat and looked out the window, rubbing his chin. 'I've not seen him for over a week. He doesn't live here anymore.'

'Will you tell me where he is?'

Penderton sat back down in his chair and poured himself another cup of tea. He opened up a canister on the table and drew out a slice of cake. 'Let me try to contact him first.' He held out a slice of cake to her. 'Then I'll contact you.'

She shook her head. 'I won't take cake, thank you. I'd better be going. Thank you for your time.' She lifted her arms to tie her loose hair back up into a bun.

Penderton studied her, and then he sucked in a breath as his eyes dropped to her throat.

'What?' she asked, dropping her hands to her lap.

Heat rushed to her cheeks at the intensity of his scrutiny.

'Where did you get that charm?'

Elena's hand went her necklace. 'I've had it since I was a baby. I think my mother gave to me.'

'Stop, wait a moment.' He got up from the table and approached her. Elena's eyes widened. He was looking at her again, studying her. This close, she could see he had green flecks in his grey eyes.

'She never told me,' he said.

'Told you what?'

He stepped back. 'About you.'

'I don't understand. Why would my mother tell you about me?'

Turning to the side, he rubbed the heel of his hand against his forehead. 'We had a thing going. A relationship. She ran away.' He shrugged, as he turned to face her again. 'Not that I blame her. I was a pigheaded fool. The whole situation was fraught. It took me a while to grow up. I never got over what happened.'

'But...Drew?'

He nodded. 'Yeah, his mother came along less than a year later. Didn't stay long. Left me the boy. That's something, I suppose.'

'I see... You must have been lonely.'

He chuckled. 'I've had the garden.'

It was true he didn't mingle much with the coven. She'd never seen him at the essential rites and festivities, though she knew him by name and had heard him spoken of.

'Aunt Elvira — '

'Yes, she hates me after what happened. She blames me for your mother running away, among other things.'

Elena had to get out. Something was going on.

She didn't quite like where this conversation was leading. She had to get help for Jake.

'Look, I have to go. Please try contacting Drew for me. This spell on Jake is serious. He is a top lawyer. The spell is affecting his judgement.' She took a few hurried steps then paused, and faced him. 'I can't let him out of my sight. I beg you to help me.'

'I will. Look...' He put his hand out, not quite reaching her. She paused, sensing he was desperate for her stay. 'You're my daughter, Elena.'

The door opened. Jake stood there. She could tell he had heard most of it. How had he snuck up the hallway without them hearing?

'You think I'm affected by a love spell?' he said in a voice that barely disguised his incredulity.

'Jake. Hi! Give me a minute, please.'

She turned to Penderton. 'Did you say I'm your daughter?' Her voice had a hysterical edge.

'Yes, I'm pretty sure. That charm, I made it for her. Traditionally, a charm like that would be given to a child of the warlock who made it. And I can see me in you, too.'

Elena's knees buckled as her world spun around her. Jake raced over, gathered her up in his arms, and then placed her on a chair. 'Can you bring her some water?' She heard him ask Penderton.

There was a gasp from Jake. Penderton had conjured a glass of water. 'Where did you...?'

Jake look flustered as he held a glass of water to her lips. This whole meeting was not playing out as she had planned. Penderton said he was her father; Jake heard about the love spell; and, to top things off, Penderton had conjured a glass of water in front of a human. Perhaps she should faint away and hope that everything resolved before she woke up.

Unfortunately, that was not how Aunt Elvira had

brought her up. She had to fix this. There was no getting out of it. She started pulling herself together.

Jake stroked her hair out of her face, his concerned eyes meeting hers. He caressed her cheek.

'Are you okay? Can I get you anything?'

She pushed out of his arms. 'I'm fine. I've had a bit of a shock, that's all.'

She looked Rory Penderton over again, looking for the parts of him that were in her. Surreptitiously, she explored his aura, wishing that it wasn't true. Yet a close blood relationship would explain why she and Drew had not taken to one another, not in a romantic sense. Sibling blood repelled. The truth hit her like a sledgehammer. 'Goddess. You're my father.' Her hand went to her mouth to cover the cry that was rising up inside her.

Jake stepped back, giving them room. Rory took his place and pulled her to him, burying his face in her neck. He controlled a sob, a hastily drawn breath full of emotion.

Controlling her own tears was difficult. She had a father. He was a warlock. She was no half-breed witch after all. All those years, and he'd lived so close, and she didn't know he was there. All those wasted years.

A flash of anger rose inside. Did Aunt Elvira know? Had she hid it from her because she hated the man? What had happened so long ago that caused all this angst?

Her father pulled back, using his thumbs to her wipe the tears from her cheeks. 'Don't cry. This is a happy moment. I may have lost my chance of happiness all those years ago, but I have you now.'

Jake shifted from one foot to another, obviously ill at ease. Rory Penderton looked over his shoulder and gestured to the vacant chair. 'Jake, I'm Rory Penderton. You may as well sit down and have a cup of tea.'

The little red teapot had steam curling out the spout again. Elena dug a tissue out of her purse and blew her nose. Her father's casual use of magic brought a smile to her face. Luckily, Jake didn't seem to notice as he sat down and poured himself some tea into a spare cup. 'I'm sorry I intruded,' he said, sheepishly. 'I should have stayed in the car.'

'Not a problem young man,' Penderton said, getting up and slapping him on the back. 'So, you're the man who is in love with my daughter?'

'Yes, I am. I want to marry her.'

Elena groaned. 'Please don't go there.' She looked fleetingly at her father. 'Can you help him?'

Jake squared his shoulders and sat back. 'I don't need any help, except to get you to say yes.'

Rory Penderton laughed, belly-laughed. 'You're right. It is a spell.' He eyed her closely, checking whether she had been affected.

'You're clear of the spell, but not unaffected by him, I think.'

Elena had the grace to blush, which brought a knowing smile to her father's face. Heavens, she thought, this is my dad. She was so confused. One part of her wanted to stay and be with him forever, and the other part wanted to go away and sort through all her feelings and come to terms with this knowledge. And then there was Jake in the mix.

'What are you talking about? I'm not affected by a spell. Forgive me for saying this, Mr Penderton, but your daughter is gorgeous. I love her. I want to be with her. Pure and simple.'

'Look, Jake, I'm sorry to say but there is a thing called magic. Someone has definitely hexed you with a love spell. I can see it, like I can see my garden out there. You need to stay with Elena until this gets sorted.'

'But — '

'Don't make any decisions. Just enjoy it.'

'There's no such thing as magic.'

'If you say so. Enjoy my daughter, in any case.' He chuckled, as his gaze shifted between them both. 'I can tell you already have been.'

Elena's cheeks flamed. 'Stop. Don't encourage him. I can't be with him, don't you understand? I would be taking advantage of him when his judgement is impaired.'

They both turned to gape at her. 'Making love with me is taking advantage of me?' Jake asked, hand on his chest.

'Of course it is. In your right mind you wouldn't want to.'

He gave her a very serious and sexy look, from the top of her head to the bottom of her toes. 'Yes. I would.'

Her gaze flicked to her father, silently pleading. 'Oh yes, he would,' he replied, with a knowing look.

'You're no help.'

Rory Penderton shrugged, but his smile had transformed his face. There was a real shine sparkling out of his eyes. He shook his head, as if he couldn't believe what he was seeing.

'I have a daughter, a beautiful daughter.' Tears trickled down his cheeks as he sunk into a chair.

'It's okay,' she said, moving toward him. Jake stood up and said he'd wait outside.

Nestled on Rory Penderton's lap, she cuddled her father, cuddled him as she would have as a little girl growing up. She didn't feel embarrassed. Those cuddles were hers, the ones she should have had her whole life.

'Will you come again?' he asked, when she kissed him on the cheek to say goodbye.

'Yes, I'd like that. But I have to sort this mess out with Jake first. Also, I need to talk to Aunt Elvira.'

'Don't be hard on her. She didn't know your mother was pregnant when she ran away. I didn't either.'

'Do you know why she left?'

'Your mother?' He shook his head. 'I thought she was angry with me, but she wouldn't have had you and left you with humans if it wasn't something more — something she hid from all of us. She was different, you know, not content with the rules of the coven...'

CHAPTER NINE

J ake sat in the car, the sound of traffic groaning behind him. He kept his gaze on the house, waiting for her to come out, to come and sit beside him. He wanted to be with Elena but knew it wasn't the right time. He didn't know the whole story, or even the reason why they were there. However, it was obvious she hadn't expected to find out that the old man was her father.

All that mattered was that he wanted her, and that the physical distance between them was painful. He wanted to touch, and feel, and be with her, inside of her, feeling her move with him. It was an ache, a long drawn-out pain that could only be eased when she was near, when their skin was touching.

The old man had talked about a spell. Elena seemed to believe it. Talk about weird Saturdays. He usually spent Saturdays working, but today he'd given it up to be with Elena. It went against the grain that, for the first time in his life he really wanted someone, and they didn't believe he was sincere. He hated that she doubted him, doubted his honesty and the depth of this feeling. He thought back to that time in the restaurant. It had been rather sudden, but his mind had already been on how much he wanted to be with her.

He'd had women before, of course: the sexy, the attractive, the vivacious, the shy, the rich, the famous. He'd sampled them all. Yet there was something about Elena that crept under his skin and crawled into his heart so fast that he really couldn't explain it.

He thought it was weird that Elena hadn't known about her father. He didn't even realise she was looking for him, but then, she hadn't talked that much about herself, not the past; only the present, the moment.

He lay back against the car seat, slid on his sunglasses and stared at the sky. He thought about the chin-up bar and how succulent she had been when he had his mouth on her. The sounds that she had made were joy to his ears. He liked pleasuring women, but he definitely loved pleasuring Elena. Recalling the moment when she had slid down his body and he had slipped inside her made him harden. She had been tight and hot and liquid. He wanted to be there again, moving inside her, enjoying the taste of her lips, her skin, her sighs.

He adjusted himself, glad the steering wheel hid his burgeoning erection. It was sweet pain to think about her.

Finally the door opened, and his gaze was riveted to her as she walked down the steps and headed back to the car. Her pink sundress and white sandals looked so fresh and young on her petite figure. Her long legs were shown to advantage by the mid-thigh length dress. His eyes lingered on her breasts, such sweet mounds, not too big or too small, perfect. How he had loved suckling on them, feeling her arch her back and surrender herself. He shook himself; he had to get a grip. He really did have it bad.

Elena opened the car door and slid into the passenger seat. He turned toward her, a smile lingering on his lips. She looked delicious. 'Where to now?'

Elena put her head back on the headrest and expelled a loud breath. She twisted her hair into a bun and slid a clip in to hold it. 'I don't know.' She turned her face toward him, her green eyes sad. 'At this moment, I don't care.'

Jake turned the key, enlivening the engine. He half-turned to reverse down the driveway. 'Okay. We'll go for a drive until you can think about what you want to do next.'

Elena nodded and did up her seatbelt. Jake couldn't think of anywhere else he would rather be than driving Elena around Sydney. Yes, he had business to do, and that was important. But Pen was holding his clients off, giving him time to come to terms with his new relationship. *God, relationship*, he thought. It was a term he'd never thought he would associate with himself. But a relationship with Elena was what he wanted.

He headed for Watsons Bay. It had a view of the harbor he wanted to share with her. From Homebush it was a long drive, but he didn't mind. He had Elena beside him.

Once on the motorway, when he no longer needed to change gears, he reached out and tucked her hand in his. The feel of her, the warmth, spread right into his heart.

He couldn't think of anywhere else to take her, not at that moment. Her Balmain semi was a great little spot and he'd love to take her home to his house in Cremorne, but he didn't think she was quite ready for that. She was already flighty and sometimes standoffish. She needed space to get accustomed to him, and the knowledge that she had a father.

That brought him to think of his own father. They had never been really close. They had an okay relationship, particularly if they stayed out of each other's way. He was the son of the second wife, and that hadn't been a good marriage. Jake had escaped to boarding school at a fairly young age, which helped minimize his mother's excesses and his father's neglect. It was how he'd learned to armor himself against love. Love had ruined his childhood, and made his parents miserable. Now, he was in love. How did that happen? How did he throw away all that caution, all that steel plating around his heart?

Yet, he had seen it happen to a number of his friends: one minute hard-hearted businessmen, and the next, smitten. He never thought it would happen to him. But in those first few minutes, as he watched her, his defenses had crumbled.

After he negotiated Sydney's infernal traffic, he made it onto New South Head Road, passing beautiful Rose Bay and heading up to Vaucluse. Sunlight glittered across the surface of the harbor. A smattering of yachts with bright sails raced with the wind. Soon they lost sight of the water as the road wound through a series of large, expensive houses, until he reached Watsons Bay. The place was parked out as usual. He was about to turn around, when a lucky departure enabled him to secure a spot.

Elena climbed out of the car and tried to repair her bun. With the top down, the wind had almost undone it completely. Giving up, she finger combed her hair, letting it fall in gentle waves around her shoulders, before dropping her clip into her purse.

He wanted to grab a handful and inhale her scent; he wanted to devour her mouth. Instead, he controlled the urge and led her across the road to the wharf so they could look out across the harbor.

What a breathtaking view it was. The water was deep aquamarine, and the cluster of Sydney's skyscrapers and the Harbor Bridge stood tall on the horizon. The harbor never failed to disappoint him, despite its moods and his.

He stood behind her. 'Lovely,' she said breathily, in a way he liked. It was as if she was finger walking up his spine. He moved closer and then gently eased her against him so that his chin could nestle on the crown of her head, and his arms swooped around to cross over on her waist.

'I could hold you all day,' he whispered in her ear. He noticed her trembling, and liked that he had that effect on her.

'I wish you could, but life will intrude eventually.'

He lowered his head and nuzzled her neck. She groaned and then stiffened before moving out of his embrace. There was an empty space where she had been.

'We shouldn't. It's only a spell.'

He chuckled at her stern look. 'I don't care.'

'You will. You'll be angry and hate me. Blame me.'

He slapped his chest. 'I swear I won't, even though I don't believe this nonsense about a spell. I'll write it down on a piece of paper. Look I'll sign it.'

Her arms were folded, her head cocked at an angle, with her chin lifted in an attitude of defiance. He wanted to kiss the frown from her brow and plunder her pouting lips.

She shook her head, sending waves of glorious hair around her shoulders. 'It's not funny. Besides, it doesn't matter, nothing you decide now would be legal. You aren't in your right mind.'

That shook him. 'Are you saying you think I'm

nuts?' The smile left his face as he examined every nuance of her face. He was pleased to see surprise written there.

'No. No! Not nuts. The spell tampers with you in a subtle way. It makes you more pliant, more able to give in. That's how the spell works, it breaks down your barriers.'

'So because of the spell I want you?' He tried to keep the sarcasm from his voice, knowing she believed what she was saying.

'Actually, I think the attraction was there from the beginning. The spell made it more, much more.'

'More what? I liked the look of you, hell, I love the feel of you. I can't see that being a spell. Except for the fact that you're bewitching me.'

Elena began to back away. 'I understand you don't believe me. That's fine. We probably shouldn't be talking about spells, anyhow.'

He lunged after her. 'Why?'

'Because it's best not to.'

'Why do you believe it's a spell? What other things have I done that you think I wouldn't normally do?'

'You grabbed my hand after meeting me all of five minutes and asked me to marry you. Does that sound like something you would normally do? You sound like a regular playboy. You sleep with women all the time, but your heart is never touched. That's right, isn't it?'

Jake rocked back on his heels. It was true. He'd never propose to a woman — well, he didn't think he would. Unless he was delusional, or he'd met the 'one'. But the 'one' didn't exist, did she?

He was ashamed about the truth in her words. He did sleep around and didn't care. He enjoyed women's bodies, enjoyed the conquest...yet something about Elena was different.

He shook his head. What was different? Her body called to him, and everything about her warmed him, sunk into him, like she was part of his fabric. Was that a spell?

'Relax, Elena. We'll see this through, okay?'

She stopped backing away from him. 'Yes, you're right. I'm getting too upset about something I can't change. It will be different from now on. I will control myself.' She nodded, and looked at him sideways. 'I'm fine now, let's go.'

He lifted his elbow away from his body so she could slide her hand there. He drew it through and patted her wrist. They headed back to the road, watching the seagulls pick up old potato chips in the grass, squawking and flapping their wings as three converged on one small morsel of food.

He leaned his head toward her catching the scent of her hair, a rosemary and herbal fragrance that made him want to sigh. 'Don't worry. It will work out. Why don't we enjoy this time? You like me, don't you?'

He caught her fleeting smile, and saw the sparkle light her eyes. 'Yes, I do. But I know it's going to end badly.'

He wanted to kiss her frown away, wanted to promise her that it wouldn't end at all, but he didn't think she wanted to hear that at present. Maybe when she got used to the idea, when she saw it was no passing fancy. 'Don't think about tomorrow. Live in the now with me, okay?'

She nodded, a smile shining in her eyes. Then she laughed.

'What?' He was enchanted by her, by the shape of her smile, and the emerald vibrancy of her eyes.

'The thought crossed my mind that it could be worse.'

He furrowed his eyebrows. 'Worse?'

'At least it's you. You're special. I like you.'

They walked on, but he couldn't help but swell with pride when she had said he was special. That sounded lovely.

'As we aren't in a hurry, shall we have some lunch at Doyle's? We can do fish and chips on the wharf or walk further down to their other restaurant.'

As they looked on, a busload of tourists poured into the wharf takeaway, making the place noisy, crowded and busy. She glanced back at him, worrying at her bottom lip. 'Perhaps the restaurant.'

'Sure, let's go. My shout.' He couldn't help the smile that spread over his face. It was one of his favorite restaurants, and they would have the opportunity to have a quiet meal together. He paused when he saw her mouth draw into a thin line.

'What?'

'I'm not sure.' She wouldn't look at him, and her cheeks flushed.

'I can afford it,' he said, before she refused outright. 'And you paid for brunch.'

She nodded and looked up with a shy smile. 'Okay then. I'd love to. I haven't been to Doyle's in ages.'

Lunch was excellent, a first course of fresh tiger prawns, followed by grilled snapper, salad and chips. They talked of inconsequential things — his love of boats, her love of craft.

'So, you don't work a real job?' he asked.

She sat back, her eyes widening at his comment. 'A real job? Isn't a real job where you earn money, enough to keep you out of debt and fed?'

He squared his shoulders. 'I didn't mean to insult you. You're bright and intelligent. I thought something professional would be more your line.'

Sitting forward, she relaxed and leaned her chin

on her hand. 'Mm. I've never thought an office was my thing. I like working the markets, meeting people and having new experiences. And I have my family. Grace is expecting, you know. I'll be an aunty soon, so I'll have other things to keep me busy.'

'So you have no ambition to get rich or travel?'

Her green eyes lit up. 'Travel? Oh yes, I want to see places, but not quite yet. Money? I need what I need to survive, and, other than that, the pursuit of money is more trouble than it's worth.'

Jake narrowed his eyes. Her lack of ambition surprised him. All the women he'd met wanted money or power, or at least to marry it. Elena wanted nothing. A gaping hole opened up inside him. What if she didn't want or need him? What if all he was, and all he had worked for meant nothing to her? How could he bear it?

She sat up and tilted her head to the side. 'What is it? Have I said something wrong?'

He shook his head, unable to articulate the desolate feeling inside him. It wasn't rational, but he couldn't fight it.

'This spell,' he asked, after taking a sip of mineral water, 'does it have any downsides?'

'Not too many that I know of, besides affecting the judgement. Euphoria, I suppose.'

'And depression?'

'I don't know firsthand, only what I learned from others.'

'So, do young witches and warlocks go to Saturday school and learn magic?' He was joking, remembering some friends who were Greek and Italian having to go to school to learn their language and culture. It always puzzled him. He never did extra classes on being Australian.

She nodded. 'They do, but I didn't. I was brought up by humans.'

'Humans?' This is good, he thought. She's going to tell me she's not human.

'Well, humans who don't have the talent, what you call magic. The folk are different from humans, and within the folk we have different species. What we have in common is talent, immunity to diseases that plague humans, and we live longer.'

'That's a relief.'

'What is?'

'Never mind.' He didn't want to take tease her, accusing her of being all 'Twilight Zoney'. Next, she'd be telling him the tooth fairy was real. He changed the topic.

'So, today with Penderton. You didn't suspect he was your father?' He was walking a fine line here, and knew that the conversation could go badly. But he wanted in, wanted her to let him past her barriers. He cared about her emotional state.

Her expression changed and lost some of its joy. 'No. I'm still trying to digest it. I was told my father was human. No one knows what happened to my mother. My aunt says she ran off and left me with a human family. It was only luck that she found me when I was thirteen.'

'Then you went to live with her?'

'Yes, and Grace. I had a good life with them. They completed me in many ways. I didn't realize I had such a big hole there where my parents were meant to be until today, until now.'

He reached across the table and squeezed her hands. 'Parents can shape us in ways we don't understand. Not all of it's good.'

Her green eyes brightened. 'I know.'

Jake felt the air grow colder and the sunlight

lessen. 'It's clouding over. Shall I take you back to your place?'

'Yes, that would be good. Thank you for your company, Jake, and the drive. It's been great spending time with you.'

He grinned for all he was worth.

CHAPTER TEN

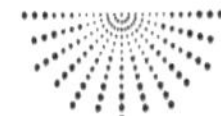

A strange woman stood by the door when they pulled up in front of Elena's house, a small overnight bag by her feet. Jake waved to the woman as he and Elena climbed out of the car.

'That's Pen. I asked her to bring me some gear from my house.'

Jake's assistant's scrutinized Elena after she had carefully taken in Jake from head to toe, and gave a nearly imperceptible nod.

'Pen. Thanks for going to all the trouble of doing this, I appreciate it.' Jake hoisted the bag and grinned.

His assistant looked askance at him. 'Sure, no problem. Hello, are you Elena? We spoke on the phone.' She held out her hand.

Elena shook the girl's cool hand and sensed that Pen was practical and careful. There was no intense emotion from her, no signs of jealousy. 'Yes, pleased to meet you in person.' Again that look assessed her, then the woman's eyes darted back to Jake. 'I'm glad the restaurant venue worked out for you both.'

Elena recalled that Pen had suggested the venue for their meeting; so how did someone else know where they'd be? She suspected Pen had set them up for an instant, but didn't pick up signs of subterfuge in the other woman. Those bright blue eyes of hers hid nothing. She wasn't the one.

'See you another time, then.' Pen waved farewell and headed to her black Mini with a red racing stripe. She opened the door and turned back to them. 'Take good care of him, Elena. He's standing on rocky ground.'

Elena lost her smile and glanced nervously at Jake. What did she mean? Could she tell he was under a spell?

Pen covered her mouth, seeing her reaction. 'Oh, I meant no offense, really. You see he never puts pleasure before business. Well done.'

Jake's expression turned stormy. 'Pen, can you keep your psychoanalysis for the office?'

Her smile was wide and knowing. Obviously, she was used to the gruff side of Jake. Her ponytail swung as she shook her head with a laugh.

'Sure I can. I'm off. I hope to see you Monday sometime. Tuesday, at the latest. After that, there are no guarantees that I can hold back the horde of clients wanting you to do some work.'

Pen hopped into her little car and sped away. Elena took in the overnight bag in Jake's hand. She guessed he'd arranged it while she was in the ladies room with Grace. It made sense that he needed clothes, and things to be comfortable, yet the thought of spending another night with him was daunting. She had to take a firm stand, or she'd be so deep she would have no control over the situation. Once was a mistake, twice was inappropriate and three times would be criminal.

She needed to talk to Aunt Elvira, urgently. *Grace? We need to talk. Is Aunt Elvira back yet?* She sent her message by hail to save time. *Grace?*

Blast, she wasn't answering. She'd call her instead, if Grace wanted to play that game. Usually they could hail within the distance of their homes.

Grabbing her keys, she moved forward to open the door. 'Are you okay?' Jake asked, as he followed her inside.

'Yes, fine. You can put your stuff in the spare room. I need a few minutes.' She picked up the phone and went to her bedroom, calling Grace on the speed dial.

'Hi, dear. I got your hail, but I was napping. What did you find out?'

'More than I expected. You?'

'I spoke to four people on that list.' Grace's voice came through slightly muffled, around a yawn. 'That's why I was napping. It took a lot out of me. Three of them were working on different potions that used the same ingredients. The other wasn't nice.'

'I'm sorry to put you through that. Thank you following those leads for me.' How did she break it to Grace about Penderton? Elena thought of a gentle way to tell her, despite the turmoil inside. If she didn't have to worry about Jake, she'd probably fall in an emotional heap. Yet she couldn't regret finding her father.

'How did you go? Did the old man hex Jake?'

'No, I don't think he did. It's possibly Drew but I can't be sure. Penderton said he hadn't seen Drew for over a week. Aunt Elvira?'

Gracie yawned loudly. The pregnancy was making her tire easily. Elena could hear the sounds she made while stretching. 'She hasn't surfaced yet. Maybe tomorrow.' Grace sounded hopeful and, at that moment, Elena wished her aunt was there for many reasons, and not only the Jake situation. She needed to know the story about her mother and Penderton. She was certain her aunt knew it all.

There was no choice but for her to sort through the mess herself. She thought back to the restaurant, to the pimply-faced waiter. Maybe she could talk to him and ask who had prepared the wine.

Yet, how did anyone know she would be there, unless they'd followed her? Still, even then it would take planning. Unless her house was bugged? She shook her head, no, not that. A warlock could have listened in on her making the appointment, though. She didn't keep wards so she wouldn't have known if they were close by, particularly if they were good at shielding themselves. It never occurred to her that someone would bother eavesdropping on her life. Perhaps they had.

Not completely convinced of her theory, she started to think outside the magical sphere. Could it be an enemy of Jake's? Maybe some very naughty warlock or witch sold their services to place the hex. She'd have to work on that possibility. She'd try Pen on Monday if the situation hadn't resolved itself by then.

Grace had started to talk. Elena shook herself out of her reverie, not realizing she'd left her cousin hanging. 'Sorry, Grace. I didn't catch that.'

'So cranky warlock is still a candidate? You don't sound yourself, what's up? Royston too much for you? Want me to come over and ride shotgun?'

'Yes, I do. Bring dinner, a movie, a board game… anything that will provide a distraction.'

'What is it? It's in your voice.' Grace had her pinned. She always knew how to wheedle information from Elena. She dreaded the next words. 'There's something you're not telling me.'

Grace's probing brought back all the memories;

the trauma of her adolescence, learning about magic, learning about herself. She let out a sudden sob, holding it back with her hand.

'Elena?'

Tears dripped down her checks to drip off her chin. 'Oh Grace. Penderton is my father.'

A sharp intake of breath and Grace exclaimed. 'What? Heavens, no.'

She sniffed loudly. 'Yes. He told me…told me he made the charm I wear. When I really looked at him, into him — oh, goddess, I knew he was too.'

Grace sighed loudly. 'That makes sense then about Drew. He'd likely make you vomit if he so much as looked at you. Hang on. I'll be there quick as I can.'

'Thanks.'

Elena hung up the phone and stared at it for a moment. Wiping her tears with the back of her hand, she sniffed noisily. About to go in search of a tissue, she noticed her door was swinging open. Jake stood there, concern creasing his brow. His look stripped away the last of her defenses. He stepped forward, opened his arms, and she threw herself onto his chest and sobbed. He'd put on a clean t-shirt, but soon it was soaking up her tears.

'There, there,' he said softly, rubbing his strong hand along her back. 'Cry it out. No point in keeping it in.'

'I'm so sorry,' she said through her sobs. 'It's such a shock. It's like half my life has been unbuckled.' She looked up at him and wiped at her tears. 'It's all folding up.' She hiccuped. 'Destabilizing…everything.'

'You are still you—beautiful and sweet. In those essentials you will never change. Finding a father only adds to your life. He seemed like a good man.'

Her eyes burned from crying. 'Yes, he did.'

No longer able to hold his gaze, she stared at his chest while trying to get her unruly emotions under control. Crying in front of someone was embarrassing. She hated it. It bared one's soul. Jake stroked her hair, and her control slipped. 'It's okay,' he said in a gentle voice. 'I'm here with you. Don't worry about a thing.' He held her until she stopped crying. 'So, Grace is bringing dinner?' he asked over her head.

She nodded against his chest and then dissolved into more tears. What else had he heard? After a few minutes, she'd had her cry out and let Jake go. Not quite able to look him in the face, she rubbed her eyes and stared at the ground. Lifting her chin, he gave her a peck on the lips, and smoothed the hair out of her eyes.

'I'll make us both a coffee. By then Grace will be here.'

She nodded and sniffed loudly. 'I'll go wash my face.'

He called to her as she was stepping into the bathroom. 'So what kind of board game is Grace likely to bring?' There was mischievous glint to his eye.

A laugh bubbled up inside of her. 'I don't know. We never play them.' Her mood lifted, and she smiled. 'It was something I threw out there — something to keep us occupied and entertained.'

'Good.' He nodded, then paused, before moving out of view. 'If you're desperate for a game to play, I have a deck of cards in my glove box.'

'Oh, what were you thinking?'

'Strip poker,' he replied his expression deadly serious.

'Oh?' Heat pooled in her belly and her face burned. Desperate to escape to the bathroom, she added, 'We'll manage without games.'

After shutting the door, she gaped at her appalling

reflection in the mirror. Her hair was standing on end, stiff from the wind. Her face was blotchy; her eyes swollen. She'd have to take a shower and hope the traces of her crying fit would fade. Jake had seen her looking like this? Gracious, how embarrassing. Another quick glance at her image and she couldn't face Grace either. She looked a mess.

F eeling refreshed and somewhat more emotionally stable, Elena entered the living room wearing pale blue track bottoms and a clean white t-shirt. The smell of coffee was enticing. Jake handed her a small cup straight away. Grace poked her head out of the kitchen.

'Dinner is in progress. Take a seat. I brought wine.'

'That's good of you, thanks.'

Jake dawdled in the kitchen, until he was shooed out by Grace. 'It's under control. Go keep Elena company. Here, take her this.' She poured some red wine into a large glass. 'This one is for you.' She extracted another glass and gave him a large portion.

Jake winked. 'You having some?'

'No. Not in my condition.' Grace patted her belly fondly and took a mouthful of orange juice.

Jake chuckled. Elena realized they were getting on well. They had an easy camaraderie that Elena envied. That was good for the evening. Not so good in the long run. There was no long run.

If only he hadn't been hexed, this evening might have been in their future.

Grace came and joined them in the lounge. The beef goulash simmered in the oven and the tantalizing aroma wafted around the room like a hearth-warming spell. Not only was Grace a talented witch, she could cook like a pro. Elena could only imitate, and right then she didn't want to try. Perhaps later she would garner the energy to open a can of peaches and scoop out some vanilla ice cream for dessert.

'Jake tells me that Rory Penderton seemed like a nice man,' Grace said, an easy smile on her face. She blinked at Elena, and sipped her orange juice.

Elena's gaze met Jake's and then slid to Grace. So they had been talking. She guessed she couldn't blame them. 'Yes, in his way. Sort of reclusive, I thought. A bit closed in, avoiding pain.'

'He's had it rough, from what I've heard. Drew's mother fairly ruined him financially, socially, and any other way she could. Didn't know your mother was in the mix, too. That surprises me.'

'Apparently Elvira is involved somehow.'

Grace's forehead creased. 'Could be. She loathes him. I wonder what happened back then. She usually likes any man. Hardly any broken bridges in her past, if you know what I mean.'

Elena nodded, she did know.

'She sounds interesting,' Jake chimed in. He inched a bit closer to Elena on the sofa. She didn't move away. Too bad if it was a spell. She'd take comfort from Jake tonight, if only the platonic kind. She was determined that he'd be sleeping on his own, though.

Grace filling them in on Declan, his new bike, the trip away and the baby, took until dinner. Grace had outdone herself, with roast potatoes cooked in garlic and rosemary to go with the tender goulash, flavored with caraway seeds. Jake complimented her cooking at least three times. Grace fairly purred at his compliments. Elena couldn't stop smiling. The food was delicious, and the meal and the company took her mind off her troubles.

Grace had brought a couple of DVDs that she thought would amuse Jake, but they had no need for them as they talked till very late in the evening. Grace kept topping up her wine glass so Elena didn't really have an idea of how much she'd drunk.

With a big yawn, Grace stood up and stretched. 'I better go now. I'll drop by tomorrow.'

Jake stood up and thanked her for the meal and her company. Elena walked Grace to the door. With her dark eyes, which missed nothing, Grace assessed Elena's face and touched her cheek lightly.

'It'll be fine. You'll see, it'll work out. Jake's great. Perhaps you can keep him. I'm sure Mother won't mind that he's human.'

Elena cast a quick look over her shoulder. Jake was picking up their glasses and taking them into the kitchen to stack the dishwasher. She turned back to Grace. 'I'm in serious trouble. I really, really like him and he is so...so...'

Grace kissed her on the cheek. 'I know.'

After the door closed, Elena paused there, staring at nothing. She had to negotiate the next half hour or so carefully, and it was going to be so hard. He'd gotten to her already. He was kind, considerate, intelligent and sensitive, on top of being hot as all hell. Rejecting his advances was going to hurt more than his pride. She shook her head. Was she even up for that?

CHAPTER ELEVEN

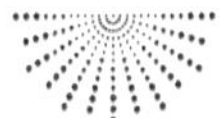

Jake came up behind her, put his arms around her and drew her close. His embrace was warm, and firm, and strong. It was so right being held like that, being held by him.

That feeling of rightness flicked on switches inside. With a sigh, she relaxed into his body. It was wrong, but his allure was too overpowering. She'd be stronger later. Maybe, when the wine she'd drunk wore off, she could spell him again — spell him good, and hope that Fel didn't come back and ruin it all by waking him up. 'Where is the cat?' she asked.

Jake let her lean out of his arms as she looked around the room. He shrugged a shoulder. 'I haven't seen it.'

There was a meow and Fel strode into the room, as if on cue.

'She must be hungry. I didn't see any cat food.'

Elena fought the wine buzz in her head. 'There's leftover goulash. I must be out of cat food.' She over-pronounced 'cat food' so Fel would take the hint. Ghost cats didn't eat.

'I'll get some for her.' Jake went into the kitchen.

Elena leaned down to speak to the cat. 'What do you think you are doing? This isn't funny.'

It's extremely amusing. I like your tom.

Her eyebrows rose. 'He's not my tom.'

'I'm sorry, did you say something?' Jake asked from the kitchen.

Elena stared blankly at him, unable to respond. He smiled at her, a brief flash of even white teeth and those intense blue eyes.

He caught sight of Fel. 'Here, kitty.'

Fel flicked her tail and waltzed into the kitchen to eat. How did a ghost cat make itself alive? *Definitely your tom*, the cat thought at her.

'What shall we do now?' Jake asked, his gaze traveling all over her, heating her blood. Elena swore she could feel a pulse in her sex. *Throb, throb.*

'Oh, well,' she said around a yawn, 'I'm going to turn in.' She went to take a step on unsteady legs, not sure if it was the wine or the arousal that was causing her loss of balance.

'Wait,' Jake said in a low, sexy voice that sent prickles along her skin and little blades of excitement trekking up her back. It was as if he had the ability to put a spell on her. She couldn't take another step and slowly turned to face him.

'Now Jake — '

He cut her off with his mouth descending on hers. His hot tongue dueled with her own as she opened to him. She melted into the kiss, but in the back of her mind she was jumping up and down and waving her hands screaming — stop it, stop it now, before it's too late. She mentally turned away from those warnings. The way he held her up close and tight, moulding her to his body, melted any resistance. His firm pecs pressed up against her taut nipples. The muscles along his back quivered as her fingers danced over them.

Free of her moral bindings, she kissed him back. Grabbing the back of his neck, she pulled him into her. Opening herself, she crushed his lips with her own, sent her tongue aggressively into his mouth and plastered her body against his. Head spinning from the dizzy contact, she backed off and licked along his lower lip. Jake shivered, and let out a low groan. He leant back, his eyes heavy with arousal. With a smile, Elena reached up and drew him down for another kiss. She wasn't fighting the spell now. She wasn't surrendering to Jake either. She was going for it, because she needed, wanted and had to have what he was offering.

Soon she was pulling up his t-shirt and trying to drag it over his head. He laughed softly at her efforts. Meanwhile, he had shoved down her track pants so they puddled around her feet, and he had his hot mouth on her left nipple, and his hand squeezing her right butt cheek. Her bra was somewhere in the vicinity of the kitchen where Jake had flung it. No, she had flung it, theatrically. He broke the kiss long enough to shuck his t-shirt.

Diving forward, Elena nibbled across his chest, lathing each nipple with her tongue, grinning when he groaned. Her hands slid down his sides, anchoring on his hips as she rubbed herself against him. In reaction to her boldness, he lunged for her neck and sucked, making her gasp before he kissed her soundly all over again.

'I love the feel in you,' he said. 'I like the way you make me feel when our skin meets, when our lips join.' His eyes rolled up. 'I love being inside you.'

The timbre of his voice slid along her nerves,

snatching her breath and kicking up her heart rate. She wanted him inside her, too.

Elena's hands strayed lower, unbuttoning his jeans and then lowering the zip gently to spring him free. She pushed his jeans down, tugging them to the floor. She knelt and helped him step out of them, reaching up to drag the boxers down too. On standing, hot taut flesh met her eager hands. He was engorged and ready. She wanted to taste him. Closing her eyes, she kissed him hard and full on the mouth.

His hands held her head as his tongue explored, enlivening her passion until she could no longer hold back.

How much wine had she drunk? Previously, she could say he outmaneuvered her, that she'd succumbed to him. But this was aggression on her part. She was actively pursuing this encounter.

She was going to be sorry. Well, if she had to pay a price, she was going to earn the punishment. Breaking the kiss, she pushed him back toward the sofa. He dropped into the seat, his eyes dark with lust. She ran her gaze over his body. Bold and naked, she stood before him drinking in his wide shoulders, narrow hips and succulent-looking cock.

He'd given her pleasure and she wanted to return it. She nudged his knees apart and settled between them, taking him in her hand. Lowering her head, she slow-licked the tip of his erection. Jake gasped. Then she took him all in, deep as she could go, cupping his balls in her hands. She licked him like he was an ice cream. She wasn't experienced, but she had read about sex. *Inexperienced, but not ignorant*, she thought as she pleasured him, egged on by the sounds he made. He called out her name and a dozen other things as she brought him close and then eased off. His reaction was turning her on, making her wet.

Sitting back on her heels, she watched as she continued to stroke him. His chest heaved, a sprinkling of sweat across his skin. His eyes were darting around as he moaned. How she loved to have this power over him. She'd never sought to be so blatant in a sexual act before. The wine had certainly lowered her inhibitions, but it was more. It was him, and how he treated her, and reacted to her. They had a secret language.

Releasing his hot cock, she grinned, knowing she had annihilated him sexually.

'Condom,' he said in a tight voice.

She looked on the floor for his boxers and tossed them over. He dug out a condom in a pincer grip. Together, they slipped on the sheath and then he caught her up in a deep kiss, until he broke it off and whispered in her ear, 'You're amazing.' It sent a shiver through her.

He grabbed her behind her thighs, easing her up. Carefully, she lowered herself down. The thrust of pleasure made her arch her back and cry out. He jerked his hips once. Her breath caught. She couldn't move; he filled her up.

The need to feel him moving inside her built. She couldn't remain, still so she rode him. His hardness stroked her. Putting his hands on her waist, he held her and took over, moving under her. His six-pack rippled with each powerful thrust. She put her hands on the back of the couch to steady herself as he bucked. Like an express train, her orgasm overtook her.

Jake changed the rhythm, slowing his thrusts so that she shuddered as he withdrew and then cried out when he thrust again. She caught the rhythm and moved with him, taking control once again.

Their gazes met. Free of her shyness, Elena leaned

down to snatch a kiss. Releasing her mouth, he snagged a nipple and suckled hard while he kept up his hypnotic rhythm. Pressure began to build again. She was powerless to hold back her next orgasm.

He growled low in his throat as he grabbed her around the waist. Again, she couldn't help but respond to his voice with a ripple of seduction that ran along her spine and made her heart beat faster, made her body surrender. He placed her sideways on the sofa. Holding her leg over his shoulder, he drove repeatedly into her. Elena was now being ridden hard. She was so aroused, her labia was thick and sensitive. The friction of his cock made her suck in excited breath after excited breath. The noise coming out of her mouth was unrecognizable.

The control had shifted. It was Jake's game now. He was pushing her beyond anything she had experienced before.

He stopped, suddenly. She had a chance to suck in several deep breaths when he withdrew. Coherent thought was way out of reach. Hormones were rampant in her system.

Guiding her to a new position on her knees with her holding the edge of the couch, he speared her from behind. Taking hold of her hips, he angled each thrust until she was groaning and crying out, her throat now hoarse. He dominated her, and the deep core of her responded. Her shatter moment was approaching fast, and it scared and fascinated her.

'Jake,' she said breathlessly. 'I can't take much more.'

'Give me a minute,' Jake said through clenched teeth.

Tremors overtook as her mind exploded with pleasure. Jake slammed into her with a roar, folding himself over her as he ground himself deep. They collapsed together onto the sofa, limbs entwined, breathing rapid and deep, as if they'd run a marathon.

Elena dozed a little in Jake's warm embrace. The wine had made her loosen up and the drowsy aftereffects hit home. Jake swore, jerking her out of her doze.

'What is it?' she asked. Reaching out, she caressed his stiff shoulders. His brow furrowed. His mouth was drawn into a thin line. 'The condom broke. I'm sorry.'

The remains of the condom resembled a tattered balloon, hanging off his semi-hard erection. Elena laughed at the sight. 'We must have been too vigorous.'

'You're not upset?'

That made her laugh some more. 'Elena?' His voice had a hard edge, but his expression was neutral, barely disguising his anger.

'Come on, Jake. It was an accident. It will be all right.' Being a witch did have benefits, which included some immunity to diseases, including sexually transmitted ones.

His brow furrowed. 'Are you sure? We could get a morning-after pill.'

'A what?'

'You know, in case you get pregnant. You take a pill that stops it.'

Jake reached for a tissue on the coffee table and dealt with the condom in swift, efficient movements.

'I see. Don't worry, I'll take care of it.' She gave him a grin.

He assessed her and nodded. 'If you're sure.'

'Of course I am.'

'Come over here then. I want to cuddle you some more.' She draped herself over him as he leaned back against the end of the couch. It was luxurious, lying naked together.

As I said, a very good tom. Fel sauntered past them.

'Rotten cat,' she said.

'What's the matter? It's only a cat.' Jake smiled, his expression sated and satisfied. 'It's not like it understands what we were doing.'

'You think so? Cats are smart — that one especially.'

He hugged her. 'That was amazing. Who cares if the cat saw us? It's not like it can tell the neighbors.'

'I wouldn't bet on it.'

Jake chuckled. 'Do you want the cat to go outside?'

'No, it's okay. She'll sleep in the spare room.'

He hugged her. 'So I get to spend the night with you? No arguments?'

'No arguments,' she agreed. Tomorrow, she'd put a stop to this. Tomorrow, she'd have moral fiber. In this moment she had none. She was hurting. Jake was offering to comfort her, and that was right and good. But the truth was she wanted him, even though it was going to end in heartbreak on her side, and anger on his.

Sleep claimed her. She woke briefly when Jake put her to bed. She muttered a thank you and then smiled when he climbed in and drew her close. She loved the feel of him beside her, loved the way she seemed to fit the contours of his body so well. This time, when they slept together, it wasn't strange, it was right. She drifted off to sleep, her brain spinning from the wine.

CHAPTER TWELVE

The sound of an occasional groan from the bathroom woke Jake the next morning. Elena sounded as if she had a slight hangover. He had held her the whole night, not wanting to let go of her. What an amazing evening. She had been so giving. It had been a while since a woman had truly tried to pleasure him. He hated the thought that she had slipped out of bed without him knowing. More lovemaking would have set him up well for the day.

He located his boxers on the floor and put them on. He slipped into the kitchen and put on the espresso machine, thinking to make them both a nice coffee. He'd caught the last dribble of black brew in her cup when Elena came into the living room.

'Coffee?' he said, and produced the cup with a flourish. He could tell there was something wrong by the way she held her mouth, and the hard look in her eyes. She shook her head, avoiding direct eye contact, as she scanned the room.

'What's wrong?' He put the coffee cup down and approached. 'Are you okay?' he said tenderly. She backed up, putting her hands up to ward him off.

He stopped, the emotional blow from her rejection wounding deep. 'What is it? Why are you acting like this?'

'I'm sorry. I can't do this. I can't be involved.' She dived on the sofa, lifted a cushion, distracted as she looked for something.

'Elena?' He hated the anguish in his voice but couldn't disguise it.

She looked up and said casually, as if she hadn't brushed him off, hadn't broken his heart, 'How much did I drink last night?' Dark rings encircled her eyes, and her skin lacked its normal glow.

Still reeling, he responded automatically. 'Two, maybe three glasses.'

'Oh goddess,' she groaned, and held her hand to her forehead. 'No wonder my head is thumping.'

He tried approaching her again. She backed up and then darted to the desk to pick up the phone. 'Don't touch me, please.'

'Why? I don't understand.'

She held the phone to her chest. 'I'm so sorry for what I did to you last night. It shouldn't have happened. I took advantage of you. I'm going to confess to the coven council. Request judgement.'

He shook his head. 'What are you talking about? Last night was amazing — you were amazing.'

Tears leaked out of her eyes. 'It shouldn't have happened. It wasn't fair to you. It was wrong of me. I should've been stronger.' She shook her head and wiped the back of her hands across her cheeks. 'Our attraction is so strong. I wasn't ready for it. I should've been protecting you.'

She covered her face with her hands, shaking her head.

He edged closer, dying to reach out and hold her to him, to make her forget the terrible words she was staying. 'It was mutual,' he said, trying to pitch his voice at a level that would help her relax. 'I wish you would forget all that spell mumbo jumbo. I want to be with you. I want you right now.'

As if startled, she stepped back again, bumping up against the breakfast bar. She threw up her hands, palms out, and shook her head emphatically. 'No, it can't happen again.'

He lunged for her and caught her around the waist. She struggled, pushing at his hands as he drew her up against his body. He tried to capture her mouth but she turned her face away. 'No, Jake. Stop.'

And he did. It was as if she'd punched him solid in the gut. He backed away from her, seeing the truth of her words in her face. She didn't desire him. Didn't want him. Didn't need him.

They stared at each other for a few moments. How could she no longer desire him? Jake had never taken anything from an unwilling woman. Her rejection ripped his heart out of his chest.

'Look, I've got a lead on who placed the spell. I'm going to call Grace. She'll come over to keep you company.'

'I want to come with you.' Was that even his voice? Surely he didn't sound so lost, so pathetic. It was as if his vibrancy had been bled out of him.

'No, that's out of the question. I'll be back —' she checked her watch ' — before lunch. We can talk more then.'

He said nothing, biting down on his misery and anger.

She lifted the phone and pressed the speed dial. After a few moments, it answered. 'I need a favor. Can you come over? Now? Sure. Excellent.'

She ended the call and placed the phone back on the table. 'I'll take that coffee now. You have time for a shower before Grace gets here.' Her voice was business-like, and hard as nails. A black cloud of depression swamped him.

Jake turned around and stumbled blindly to the bathroom. Her manner was so perfunctory. He couldn't believe it was the same woman who had made love so passionately the night before, the woman who had given of herself to please him. His impulse was to grab her and force her to come back, to be the Elena who had a smile around her eyes when she looked at him. This Elena was cold. This Elena did not love. He couldn't bear the thought of that.

The rational part of his mind argued with him. *Come on, mate. You've never taken rejection like this. You've been broken up with before, get a grip.* But there was something inside of him, a rot that festered with dark emotion, self-pity, and oozed despair.

He placed his head on the wall of the shower and let the water fall about his shoulders. The emotions inside him erupted. He couldn't live without her. He didn't want to live without her. Only her love mattered.

Tears joined with the droplets falling from the shower head. He wiped his cheek, surprised by them. He hadn't cried since he was thirteen. Not since both his parents forgot to pick him up from school at Christmas. He'd spent Christmas day and the rest of the holidays alone at school, feeling as empty as an undecorated Christmas tree, knowing he'd been forgotten, not cared about, and was totally alone in the world.

Drying off, he checked his face in the mirror as he shaved. He looked the same, but there was something missing. There must be something wrong with him if she no longer wanted him. What could it be?

He dressed in jeans and a pale-blue shirt and stole into the lounge room, hoping it had been a mistake and that the Elena he loved was back. When he saw Grace sitting on the sofa with no sign of Elena, his mood hit rock bottom. It was as if his heart had been cut out and handed to him. It was all he could do to stay upright.

Emotion roiled within him. He let out a gasp. He wanted to fold himself into a fetal position and make the world go away. Pinpricks of tears stung his eyes. He blinked, fast, fighting the urge to lose it right then.

'Hi,' Grace said, as she turned with a smile and waved in the general direction of the kitchen. 'I've made a fresh batch of coffee. Elena will be back soon.' She flicked open a home decorating magazine and started to read.

When he didn't answer, she put it down and looked at him sideways. He was still trying to come to grips with his inner turmoil. She climbed to her feet and approached him. 'What is it?'

Jake did his best to appear calm. When their eyes met, her brow furrowed. 'You look like shit.'

He nodded, not quite able to get any words out, afraid that if he said what he was thinking and feeling he'd burst into tears and wail like a girl.

Grace looked him up and down, a hand on her hip. 'Wait a minute. Something is not right. Either you're really hung-over, desperately ill or…let me check you out.'

Her hands hovered by the side of his head and then followed a vague outline of his body. Her eyes closed and she bit her lower lip.

He didn't want her close to him. He wanted Elena, and that want allowed him to speak.

'What are you doing?' Nice as Grace was, he

didn't want her invading his space. He didn't like the mumbo jumbo stuff either, waving hands, talking about spells. It made him cringe. He held himself still, even when his instinct was to step back. Despite how miserable he was, he didn't want to offend her. She was in his corner.

'Checking this spell. Oh dear. That's not good.' Eyes dark with concern, her mouth drew in a straight line.

His despair made his temper fray. He'd had enough of the damn spell business.

'What are you talking about? You two are daft. There's no such thing as magic.'

Grace chewed her lip and lifted a sardonic eyebrow. 'I wish that were so. How are you feeling right now?'

He walked past her into the kitchen, grabbing the cup of coffee she'd prepared. He battened down all the hatches on his emotions, except a few slipped beneath his control — anger and frustration.

'I feel like shit. I'm angry and I'm…'

'What?' she asked as she stood on the other side of the breakfast bar, her dark eyes seeing more than they should, her sympathy drawing out the inner tangle of his emotions. It was as if she'd found his thread and was relentlessly tugging.

'Desolate.'

'And?'

'Sad. God!' He searched for another word. 'Empty?'

'Uh-huh.' Grace was nodding in a knowing way, her expression sombre. 'And?'

'Like I'm nothing, that life is nothing.'

Grace bit her lip. 'That's what I thought.'

'What?' He scowled at her. 'How could you know all that?'

'The spell. It's gone bad.'

'Don't start on that again.' He stalked into the living area.

Following, she shook her head. 'Please, humor me. Tell me what happened.'

Emotion swamped him, and he staggered backward towards the sofa, sat down hard and dropped his head into his hands. 'She. Rejected. Me.'

Grace's soft hands ran over his hair as she sat next to him. 'Tell me the rest.'

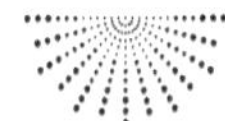

Elena stepped out of the taxi and headed into Hotel Vive. Inside, it was quiet, with a few patrons taking coffee or late breakfast. She walked around, keeping her eyes out for the pimply-faced waiter. About to give up, she spotted him polishing cutlery in a dark corner of the room.

Heading straight over, she slowed as she neared him. 'Hello. Excuse me, I was wondering if you had a minute.'

He stood up straight and put down the handful of forks he was holding, his eyes rather wide with surprise. He'd been a world away. 'I'm sorry. Do you need something?' he said, standing on the balls of his feet like he was going to dash off.

She lifted her hand as if to hold him. 'No, only some information. The night before last, I was here with someone. Maybe you remember.'

He lifted his head, his eyes tracking down her body. 'Maybe.'

'I was with a tall, well-built man. I spilled my wine, which came in a cut-crystal glass.'

Recognition lit his eyes. 'Yes, I remember.'

She nodded. 'Now, do you remember who poured the wine?'

He cupped his chin and titled his head to the side. 'It wasn't me. I was on tables. There was a new guy at the bar. Yeah, I remember now. It was weird, because he quit straight away. Didn't even last his first shift.'

Anticipation made her breath catch, her voice eager. 'So do you remember what he looked like? Could you describe him?'

'Is there a problem? I'm not sure I should tell you anything else. I might get in trouble.' His body stiffened and his expression grew wary.

'It's all right. You won't get into trouble. I thought it was someone I knew. You know when you have a name on the tip of your tongue and can't quite remember what it is.'

The waiter relaxed, easing his tense shoulders, his mouth losing its thin line. He was going to tell her. Too bad her talent didn't extend to mind reading; that way she could have taken what she wanted directly.

'Can't tell you his name, unfortunately. He was just under six foot, dark hair and eyes, and kind of surly.'

Rats. Sounded like Drew. Then she remembered she had a photo of him on her phone from their one and only date. 'Wait.' She thumbed through her images. 'Is this him?' She held out the phone.

'Yes, that's him.'

'Thank you so much. Also, I forgot to leave a tip. I really appreciated your good service the other day.' She dug out a ten dollar note and placed it in his hand. 'Thank you again.'

It was no comfort to her that it was actually Drew Penderton who had hexed Jake, but at least they had something to go on.

As Elena walked out of the hotel, her mobile phone rang. She didn't recognize the number.

'Hello?'

'Elena?'

It was her father. Butterflies took flight in her stomach. 'Hi. How are you?'

'Fine. I thought I'd ring to see how things were going with the hex. Any developments?'

Elena scanned the traffic, hoping to catch a cab. She checked her watch. A ferry was due in ten minutes, so she began walking toward the quay. 'Royston is still affected by the spell.'

'Jake is a Royston?'

'Yes, why?'

He hesitated. 'Nothing important. Any leads on who did it?'

She bit her lip, hesitating. She could imagine the hurt. She didn't know the full story of what passed between father and son, but she had developed a soft spot for Rory Penderton. She was pretty certain that he wasn't involved in the placing of the hex. 'Yes. I'm sorry, but it was Drew. I've had confirmation that he was working at the hotel. He served the wine and quit straight after.'

'What?'

'We need to find him, fast. I need to get Jake back to his old self and back to work by tomorrow. Drew has to remove the hex.'

Penderton let out a groan. 'Are you absolutely sure it's Drew?'

Elena understood that he didn't want to believe it, didn't want to accept. 'Yes, I showed the waiter that served us a photo.'

'That does place him in the prime suspect spot, doesn't it?' Rory let out a sigh, but didn't speak. Elena didn't have time for the delay.

'Yes, it does. Please, I need to find Drew.'

Rory grunted. 'I don't know where he is. We didn't part on the best of terms. I'll do what I can, chase up a few leads.'

Elena ended the call, and her phone rang again straight away. It was Grace. A tremor passed through her. She stopped walking and held her stomach; the butterflies had turned to pecking crows. It was bad news. Grace couldn't stop her negative vibrations reaching her.

'Grace?'

'He's gone. I'm sorry but he tricked me.'

Elena knees weakened. 'What do you mean he tricked you and he's gone?'

'The spell went bad. He's so depressed about what happened with you this morning. I think he's suicidal.'

'What?' She remembered how cold she'd been. She had no idea he was so fragile, that her rejection had really wounded him. Maybe that was what she told herself, so she wouldn't feel bad. If anything happened to him, she'd be heartbroken. Who was she kidding? She was heading smack into a wall of heart-break regardless, with no functioning brakes.

'He hit rock bottom,' added Grace. 'There wasn't anything I could do to make him feel better.'

She shook her head. 'How can that be? He's so strong-minded, a hard ass lawyer.'

'It's the spell. It went bad.' Grace's voice took on a lecturing tone.

'I didn't know a love spell could do that.'

Grace let out a long, sad sigh. 'They can. Learned it in school.'

Elena ground her teeth. She'd missed out on that training, and was suffering for it. Now it looked like Jake would, too. 'Why didn't you say something?'

Grace gave a low growl of irritation. 'I tried to this morning, but you were so het up and angry that I couldn't get a word in. I didn't realize Jake was bad until you had gone. He was devastated by your rejection. Why did you do that?'

'You know why.' A passer-by looked up at the tone in her voice. She turned away and walked toward a wall. 'I couldn't continue to take advantage of him. You don't know what I did when you left last night. I...drank too much. I just went with it. Seduced him. I've sought judgement from the coven council.'

Grace didn't bother masking her groan of exasperation. 'You what? No one is going to get upset about this. You didn't cast the spell. You're the victim.'

'Grace, I don't see it that way.' Pending disaster loomed, and she was caught up in it. She'd caused Jake hurt and no amount of apologizing was going to fix it.

'Well, you're wrong. Now it's a bloody mess. You like him, Elena. Maybe you're in love with him. How could you hurt someone you care about? It's not like you.'

As she replayed the scene from this morning, her gut churned. She'd avoided looking him in the eyes, not wanting to see his pain. She'd been brutal and cold while he'd been vulnerable and exposed. That was probably worse than enjoying his body. At least in that she couldn't help herself. Her rejection had been deliberate. She was angry at her own weakness, and took it out on him. She held her hand to her forehead. 'Okay, I hear you. What happened?' She paced, and then had to stop to avoid colliding with another pedestrian. Being Sydney, the man kept walking and didn't appear to notice she was having a crisis phone call.

'When he found you had left, it was like the life drained out of him. I saw that the spell was going bad. You know how the spell amplifies feelings of attraction? Now it's magnifying feelings of rejection. He couldn't cope with your brush off. I tried to talk him around.'

'And then what? He stormed out?'

'No, no. I spelled him a little, so he'd take a nap until you came back. He seemed to succumb. Although when I checked the spare room an hour later, he'd snuck out.'

Elena ground her teeth. She hoped that he'd gone to the office rather than somewhere else. Then she had a thought. 'Grace, your sleep spell is pretty strong. Are you sure you spelled him?'

She could hear Grace grinding her teeth. 'Of course I did. But only a light one. He should have stayed under for at least two hours. But it is rather odd that the sleep spell slid off him so easily. It's like he has some immunity and that's, well...maybe the spell going bad interfered with my magic. But that hasn't happened before. How weird...'

'Grace, pay attention. Do you know where he is, or where he might go?'

'I don't know. The car is gone. He's gone.'

'Can you track him?' Elena's heart was beating frantically. Grace had such a range of talent. It was her best hope of finding him.

'I tried already, but he is under my radar.'

'Okay. Try this. Get the coven to scout for Drew — better still, find his mobile number. Someone must have it. We have an emergency on our hands.'

'So it was Drew?'

'Yes. We need to find him ASAP. This could turn nasty.' Elena's tears stung her eyes. A wrong decision could ruin Jake Royston's career. Suicide would ruin his life. She tried not to entertain the possibilities.

'Okay. I'll hail Robertson. He's lead councillor this month. I'll get him to do the round up. Together, they should be able to hail mother, get her attention. I'm sure after that they will look for both of them. I'll call you when I hear something.'

'I'll try to find Jake. I'm near his office.'

Around the corner, the AMP building loomed above her. Jake's office was located on the 35th floor. As it was Sunday, the offices were closed. Elena had never broken into a building before. She wasn't familiar with the tech.

In the street, she looked around for Jake's car, then realized he was likely to have a car space inside the building. She navigated around the block, discovering that the parking entry was on the other side.

Metal roller doors covered the entrance to the car park. No easy entry for a pedestrian without an access card. Standing in the driveway with her hands on hips, she jumped when a car tooted behind her.

Moving out of the way, she watched the driver trigger the doors. Maybe she could sneak in behind, tailgate. She had to adapt a spell that would leave the image of her standing there so the driver wouldn't see her sneak in. Again, she regretted her lack of talent. This spell would tax her, but she could do it. She had to do it, create a freeze frame image of herself standing outside, and hold it long enough for her to dash inside along the shadowed wall.

The red tail-lights glowed in the dim light. The driver hadn't noticed her sneaking in so her shadow spell must have worked. Resting inside in a dark niche in the wall, she waited a few minutes to gain her strength. The spell had left her weak.

Wiping sweat from her forehead, she wrinkled

her nose. The smell of urine was very strong near the entry ramp, no doubt courtesy of late night revelers relieving themselves while they waited for buses or cabs. Not able to stand it any longer, she was grateful to find the smell of urine decreased the further she moved away from the entry. Her strength returned after a few minutes and she moved on.

The sound of her footsteps echoed against the concrete floor and walls. Now she was inside the building, she needed to confirm Jake was there before trying to get to his office, and that meant finding his red BMW.

There were a few cars on the first level, but none were Jake's. From there, a ramp spiraled down. On the next level she peered around a large, concrete pillar to scan the cars parked there. There was no sign of Jake's car.

She reached the next level. A fluorescent light flickered above her head. She peered into the dimness around her. There was a red car, and her heart beat faster. As she neared it, she found it wasn't Jake's, and her mood crashed.

Her phone rang, sounding overly loud in the quiet space. She took it out and looked at the caller ID.

'Finally,' she said as she accepted the call. 'Aunt Elvira. Nice to hear from you.'

'Elena,' Aunt Elvira said in her smooth tone. 'What is going on? Grace told me the most extraordinary thing.'

Elena blinked as she wondered which extraordinary thing. She didn't think Grace would tell her mother about her father.

'Elena?'

'I'm here. What thing?'

Elvira took in a huge breath. 'My stars. It's true then. All of it?'

'Aunt…'

'Drew Penderton hexed the lawyer, nearly hexed you?'

'Yes, I believe it was Drew.'

'What are you doing now?'

'I'm looking for Jake.'

'Everyone is. Not easy in this city. It's full of people.'

'Perhaps you'd have better luck finding Drew. You have talents in that area.' Elvira was highly skilled in the art of tracking people. 'Perhaps you could start with his father.'

The phone went silent.

'Aunt?'

'I heard you. I can't stand that man. There is no way on this earth I am going near him.' Elvira's voice was a hiss of distaste. Grace had not spilled those beans.

Elena rolled her eyes. 'You wanted me to have babies with his son. Believe me, the son is much worse than the father.'

'It wasn't quite like that… You've been to see him?' There was a slight edge to her aunt's voice.

'Yes, I have. Look, I have to go. Call me when you have something.'

'Fine. I'm looking. I'll try to hone in on Drew.'

Elena ended the call, doing her best not to shake her fists at the ceiling. Elvira decides to turn up now after being so unavailable, and then refuses to even speak to Rory Penderton, despite their predicament. She'd have it out with the old witch soon enough. She'd had enough with these games and petty dislikes; Jake's life was at a stake.

Elena continued walking around that level of the car park. There was nothing else in the flat flickering light, except a pink Jaguar.

Descending to the next level, her hope dissolved. Here she imagined the weight of the building pushing down on her. She was far from sunlight and far from warmth. She walked around the pillar and pulled up short, sucking in a huge breath.

It was Jake's car. Empty. Lonely. Red.

Elena's heart thumped hard in her chest, almost causing her pain. He was there. She had to confront him.

Turmoil fed the anxiety she was feeling. She shouldn't care about him, but she did. She should have been stronger and not let the relationship get this far, but there was nothing she could do about that now. She thought about that morning, and the look in his eyes when she had so hard-heartedly rejected him.

She'd thought she was doing the right thing; she hadn't known the spell was going bad didn't know it could. Now that rejection was causing him harm, she was even more culpable than before. If anything happened to him, it would be her fault. If anything happened to him, she'd die of a broken heart. What was she thinking? A broken heart was the least of her worries. He'd probably sue her ass.

She checked around the car park, looking for a way into the building. The lift didn't arrive when she pressed the button, so it was obviously locked down. She looked around for the stairwell. She found one, locked up tight. Groaning in frustration, she swung around, looking for another way in.

There was a stairwell on the other side of the building. She ran over to it. A little card stuck out — the kind of card you see when security had checked the doors, except this one appeared to be stopping the spring latch engaging. She leaned on it. The card dropped to the ground as the door opened. She was inside the stairwell. Looking up, she realized she had a long way to go and not much time.

Taking off her sandals, she held them in her hand and started to climb the stairs. The stairwell was dimly lit. The concrete was cool under the soles of her feet. After about ten flights, her calves started to cramp. The trim on the risers had begun to rub against her bare soles. To soothe her hurt, she let out some healing magic and continued up.

Occasionally she heard a clang and a rumble as the elevator engaged. She hoped it wasn't Jake leaving the building while she was climbing up the stairs. Not that she didn't deserve such torture, given her behavior. Perhaps she could reach out, like Grace did, and try to see if it was Jake. She stopped still and concentrated. There was nothing there, as far as she could feel. Nothing that resembled the strong personality of Jake Royston.

Returning to her slow climb, she wondered why she hadn't heard anything from the coven. Surely someone knew something by now and could give her an update.

She dragged out her mobile phone and glanced at the display. There were hardly any bars. The metal and concrete impeded her phone's efforts to get a clear signal. She sped up; she needed to get to level thirty five really quickly. She had a bad feeling.

Finally, level thirty five was reached. Elena fretted that the door would be locked. She turned the handle and it opened. Giving silent thanks to the deities, she slipped into the carpeted hallway. Still holding her shoes in her hand, she wandered around the corridor looking for a sign that read Jake Royston and Associates.

The phone rang as she was tugging on the locked

door. She slapped her palm against the thick glass panel. He wasn't there.

'Hello?' It wasn't a number she knew. But as she had mobilized the whole coven, anyone could be ringing her.

'Elena? This is your father. I have news. I've contacted Drew. I'm texting you his number. I'm afraid he hasn't admitted anything, doesn't believe what we discovered, that you are brother and sister. He thinks I'm saying it to lessen the dent to his pride.'

'Thanks…Dad.' As tense as she was, she liked the sound of that 'Dad' in her mouth. It was something she never thought she'd say.

'Where are you?' he asked softly, concern in his voice.

'In Jake's building but he doesn't appear to be in his office.'

Her phone began to vibrate, signaling another call was coming in. 'Look I have to take another call.' She didn't even say goodbye before she hit the button.

'Yes?'

It was Grace. 'Elena. Jake's on the roof of his office building. We think he is going to jump. How far away are you?'

CHAPTER FOURTEEN

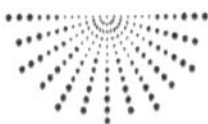

Elena nearly dropped the phone in her haste to run to the stairwell. She pulled up short in front of the elevator. She pressed the button repeatedly but it wouldn't light up. She glanced around and saw she needed a security pass. 'I'm on the 35th floor outside his office. I'll keep heading up. Penderton is sending me Drew's number. I'll send it on. We've got to put a stop to this.'

'I'll let the others know what you're doing,' Grace replied before hanging up.

In a hurry, Elena left her shoes outside Jake's office and re-entered the stairwell. She had another nine flights to go. As she ran up the stairs, she prayed she wouldn't be too late.

Elena checked her messages. Drew's number had not arrived. Damn network reception was weak in the stairwell still.

Her faster pace was not doing her muscles any favors. Shaking her head in disgust at her own weakness, she pushed little bit more magic into her muscles. It was enough to relieve the immediate pain as she took the stairs at two at a time. The messages would have to wait until she reached the roof.

A wave of relief hit her as she made the final floor, and reached the door that opened out onto the roof. It was hard to push open. There was a strong wind coming in from the harbor. She shoved, and the door flew out of her hands when a gust caught it.

'Jake!' she called. The wind snatched the words out of her mouth and twisted her hair around her face.

Clinging to the wall, she edged around the staircase housing to see if she could spot him while dragging hair out of her eyes and mouth. The huge air conditioning unit blocked her view so she crept around it, swinging her head to keep her windblown hair from impeding her vision. Then she saw the view. Her knees trembled at how high she was, and how precarious her foothold with the wind buffeting her.

Jake stood by railing on the other side of the building, looking out across Circular Quay. She brought her phone close to her face as Drew's number flashed up. She forwarded it onto Grace. She couldn't do two things at once. She needed to talk to Jake before calling Drew.

Jake was awfully close to the edge. It was a long way down. When she took a step in his direction the wind grabbed her dress, making it fly up. She held on to it as she made her way over. A sharp gust nearly knocked her off her feet.

'Jake,' she called.

This time he heard her, and turned around. Elena stood stock-still, shocked by how much his face had changed. As well as an emotional effect, the spell going bad had physical repercussions. His eyes were encircled with dark shadows, his cheeks sunken and drawn. 'Stay where you are.' Even his voice sounded empty.

'Jake, I'm sorry. I didn't mean what I said.'

His intense gaze held her. 'It's too late now.'

'No, not too late. I'm here. I can make it right. Please.'

He shook his head. She could tell her words had no effect. It was as if his skin was ice and she was sleet sliding off him.

'It's over. It doesn't matter.'

Choking back a wail, she protested, 'No, it's not over. It does matter. Please forgive me.'

He shook his head again and used his hand to chop down empathically. 'There's nothing to forgive. You see, I know. I know I don't matter.'

Elena let out a growl. She wanted to kick and scream and rant at him, at anyone. How wrong were these words coming out of his mouth? These thoughts and feelings were not natural to him. He had drive and stamina and ambition, and this spell had taken it out of him and screwed it all up into something miserable, something without hope.

'It does matter. I know you don't believe me about the spell but it's true. It's not you feeling this way. It's the spell. It's gone bad; it's festering inside of you.'

'What does it matter to you why I feel this way? You don't care.'

She took an impulsive step toward him. 'I do care.' He grew rigid and wary. She pressed her point. 'Would I be here talking to you if I didn't care? Goddess, I'm so far gone on you, I can't think straight. I seduced you because I wanted you. I was so remorseful about it afterwards, but not because I don't care for you. I was wrong to take advantage of you. I wish there was no spell, that you could love me honestly and truly.'

His features stayed perfectly composed in that state of misery and wretchedness she'd found him in.

There wasn't even a hint of a smile at her declaration. She was running out of ideas, and logic didn't seem to be working. 'Please listen to me, Jake. I do care. I'm afraid, being up here on this building. I'm here for you.'

His eyes traveled from her head to her toes. She couldn't tell what emotions were there inside him. She'd have to be touching him to do that.

'Prove it,' he said. There was a trace of the Jake she knew in that command.

Elena looked at the sky for inspiration. How was she going to prove that she loved him? Nothing came to mind, so she had to ask. 'How? Will you let me come over there to be near you?'

He shook his head. 'No.'

'What then? What can I do to prove what I say?'

'Take off your bra.'

'What?'

The wind had whipped up. She wasn't quite sure what he'd said.

'Take off your bra. Toss it.'

If she wasn't so scared, she would have laughed. Typical Jake; it was a reference to his strip poker suggestion from the previous night. Would he always get his way, no matter what? At least it was better than, 'Throw yourself off the building to prove yourself.'

When she didn't move straight away, he turned from her and leaned over the side of the building. 'No! Wait,' she cried out.

She started fumbling with her clothes. 'I'm doing it. Give me a minute.'

He held onto the rail and turned towards her, the wind making his short dark hair stand on end.

It wasn't easy to get the bra off while she was still wearing her sundress. She had to put her handbag down, and her phone. After she unclasped it, she got the straps off her shoulders and pulled them over her elbow. Lifting her hand under the skirt of her dress, she reached up and tugged the bra off. She brandished the orange and lace confection before him, and then tossed it as he'd requested.

He was looking at her. She knelt down and pressed Drew's number. She was desperate to fix this. 'Can you step away from the barrier?' She watched him take a step toward her. The tightness in her chest lessened.

'I'm trying to get this spell fixed. Give me a moment. I need to speak to this jerk on the phone.' She held up a hand, fingers splayed. 'Please, five minutes, that's all I'm asking.'

He nodded, and then looked around him. It was as if there was nothing to interest him. His gaze returned to her bra and his face clouded. Was that longing in his expression?

Drew picked up. 'Elena.'

'Yes, it's me. You've got to remove the spell.'

'Why would I do that? You're having so much fun.'

So the bastard had been eavesdropping on her apartment. She hoped he got a lot out of it. May he live to regret it.

'Look, I can't talk about that now. You need to take the spell off — it's gone bad. He's going to jump off a building. He is suicidal.'

'That's odd. What did you do to him? Never mind, I think I know. You turned all cold-hearted bitch on him, didn't you?'

She closed her eyes. His criticism stung. 'I rejected him, yes.'

'Why, for goddess sake? From what I could tell you were really enjoying it. Really enjoying him getting into you. Are you so chicken-hearted, then?

Afraid he might want companionship, a commitment, children?'

'Not chicken-hearted, you bastard. I was enjoying being with him, but it was wrong. He wouldn't have wanted me without the spell.'

Drew had the audacity to laugh. 'You think?'

Elena rubbed her forehead and snuck a look at Jake. He'd taken a step away from the barrier and was watching her warily.

She smiled reassuringly. He frowned back at her.

'Hang on a minute,' she said into the phone.

'Jake?'

He was stepping backwards. He was in danger of falling over the railing. 'Stop!'

Her hand extended toward him, even though the difference was too great.

'I want to see them?'

'Them?'

'Your breasts. When I said to take off your bra it was so I could see your breasts. If you loved me, you would do this.'

Groaning, she put the phone on speaker and knelt down, making out like she was taking off her dress. 'Drew, this is very serious. The reason I didn't go for you is that we have a blood bond. You have heard that siblings get sick, nauseated, if they try to be romantic? I met your father. He is also my father. Please, for your father's sake, stop this.'

Her voice was muffled as she tried to work out how to take off her dress. She had one failed attempt lifting the skirt over her head. 'What are you doing?' Drew asked.

Elena ground her teeth. She wanted to scream at him, but losing it wasn't going to make him listen. 'I'm taking off my dress on top of this building to stop this man from ending his life because of your stupid, vindictive spell. End it now.'

She hung up. There was no point continuing. She'd have to stand to get the dress off.

Jake's gaze was fixed on her she took a couple of steps closer. 'I'm taking my dress off now. No more distractions.'

She kept her gaze on him, hoping to keep him focused on her. Perhaps he'd be tempted to step forward and touch her. The dress came up when she tugged it. The garment eased over her head, and she tossed it. A gust of wind billowed the skirt and then swooped the whole dress over the side of the building. Great, she thought. I'm in my undies in the middle of the city. Getting home is going to be fun.

Jake's gaze roamed all over her. 'You're so beautiful. Looking at you is painful.'

He turned away suddenly. She lunged forward. 'No, please. Touch me. I want you to touch me. I will be with you as long as you want me.'

Facing her again, he held out a hand. She reached for him, closing her eyes, when their fingers touched. Thank the goddess. 'A few more steps, Jake.'

She brought his hand toward her, placing it so that he cupped her breast. A ghost of a smile played around his lips.

Stepping back she brought him with her. He moved forward, his gaze locked with hers and then stopped. There was such devotion in his eyes, and sadness too. How she hated to have that power over him. The spell had definitely gone bad. He may have had the puppy dog expression before, but not this 'I live because you notice me' look.

His hand was cool on her breast. The wind whipped up her hair. She wanted to spill her heart to him. Then something moved, something within her perception, like a tug. Drew had removed the spell.

Jake stumbled, like he'd had a moment of faintness. His hand dropped from her breast and went to his forehead. He staggered, but kept his feet. Then he shook himself like a dog shaking off water.

When he looked up at her again his gaze was hard. He gaped at her, and then took in his surroundings: the large metal shed that housed the air-conditioning units, the hub of the elevator and the breeze that tugged at his clothes and hair. His eyes traveled down her next-to-naked body, furrows marring his brow.

'Jake?'

He let out a roar and fell to his knees, his voice full of misery. Elena jumped, despite herself. Leaning over, he put his hands on the ground and dry-retched. He was in that space where he had all the memories of the last few days, but they were being viewed by his normal self. It must have been strange for him. A hard light licked his eyes as he angled his head toward her. Jake looked around him, shook himself one more time as he gazed out to the harbor, his expression distant.

'What happened?'

A heavy sigh escaped her. 'Drew ended the spell.'

Shaking his head he rubbed his temples. 'I feel like shit. I can't put it all together — the last couple of days.'

'I hope you'll feel yourself again soon.'

He let out a heartfelt groan. It made goosebumps erupt on her skin. The aftermath must be bad.

She reached for him but he waved her off. 'Don't touch me.'

His gaze raked over her and then speared out

over the side of the building. She could see the bewilderment, the tremors of his anger.

'I wanted to end it. I was so…' He seemed lost. He looked around, his expression full of revulsion.

Shaking his head, he ran his hand over his head. 'Did you drug me or something?'

'No. I…' She wanted to say she had done nothing, that it wasn't her fault, but couldn't in all justice say so. She'd taken advantage of him, hurt him when he was vulnerable. 'I didn't put the spell on you. My actions didn't help. I'm sorry.'

'You still going on about that spell. You're nuts. Just leave me alone.'

The wind picked up and she hugged herself.

'Why don't you get dressed?" he asked her, shoulders stiff, fingers clenched.

'My dress blew away.'

His gaze scanned the rooftop. He nodded, rubbing his hand along his jaw. After glancing at her once under the shade of his dark brows, he climbed to his feet and shrugged off his jacket. Wordlessly, he handed it to her, and then scraped his t-shirt over his head and tossed it to her, too.

'You look cold.' There was no warmth in his voice. The chivalry was instinctive. Damn it all. She worked her head and arms into his clothes. Trying not to read too much into it, she admonished herself. Once she'd pulled the t-shirt on, she grimaced. It smelled of him. She closed her eyes, fighting the memories that the scent evoked.

'What about you?' she asked.

'I've spare clothes in my office.'

He wouldn't allow her to approach. She couldn't tell what he was feeling using magic. His forehead was clouded with anger and every movement and expression confirmed it, from the hard slant of his mouth to the clench of his jaw. His eyes, though, were the worst — the blue had turned to grey ice.

'Can we go inside, please?' she asked, hugging the jacket to herself, glad of the sweep of the t-shirt along her upper thighs.

After taking in the roof again, he nodded. A sigh left him as he began to walk toward the door. He rolled his shoulders. She couldn't help noticing his shoulder blades moving under the smooth skin of his back and the curve of the muscles of his upper arms.

As they walked together, she felt a sense of control emanating from him now, the vulnerability buried. He was probably filing the whole episode away under delusion or drug-induced psychosis. Hopefully, by the end of the day it would be a faint recollection, filed away in his logical, legal mind. It was all right for him. She had to live with the memories.

He held the door for her. 'We're done. I want you out of my life.'

The sting of tears made her blink. She wouldn't fall to pieces in front of him. He had every right to be angry, and yet this was the moment she had been trying to avoid. She could forgive his anger, could forgive him hurting her, but couldn't forgive herself falling in love with him. That had been stupidity.

Jake had a security pass so he could access the lifts after-hours. He said nothing to her, didn't even look at her while they rode the lift.

He stopped the lift suddenly. 'What are you do-ing?' she asked.

'I've changed my mind. I was going to take you to my office first. Now, I'm taking you downstairs so you can leave.' He punched the lift button.

'But...we should talk more. I can explain.'

He looked at her, anger drawing his lips thin. 'No,

you can't. I want you gone. Don't you understand? You made me believe you cared. It wasn't real. It was some kind of sick joke.'

'I do care. I'm so sorry about all of this. Please believe me.'

He straightened as the lift hit the ground floor and the door flew open. 'I don't believe anything you say. You need help, Elena. Serious help.'

Tears blossomed in her eyes as she stepped out of the lift. She didn't want him seeing her cry so she turned her head away. She deserved his anger, his scorn. She was lucky he hadn't called the police. She wasn't sure on what charges, but he was a top lawyer, so he could probably come up with something.

The green marble flooring of the building's reception area was cool under her tender feet. A lone security guard looked up from his desk and stared. Jake's jacket came to just below her buttocks. She held it around her shoulders so that the sleeves were loose. Thankfully, the t-shirt came lower and provided some sense of decency. She adjusted her handbag, keeping the phone inside, and stopped before she reached the doors. Jake didn't even check his stride.

She quickly put on the jacket correctly and buttoned it up. If she were lucky there might a taxi, or maybe she could summon someone from the coven quickly. She hoped Drew kept out of her way because she was quite ready to scratch his eyes out.

Jake held the door open for her so she could pass in front of him. She turned around, trying to see some warmth in his expression. He wouldn't even look at her and turned away.

'Jake, please.'

He hesitated, but didn't turn around. 'I'm sorry. I really am sorry I hurt you. I like you. This isn't easy for me either.'

'Yeah, well aren't you to be pitied. See you.'

He shut the door and it locked behind him automatically. She stood there, watching him growing smaller as he walked along the foyer and re-entered the lift.

The sounds of traffic passing behind reminded her that she was standing in the middle of Sydney, partially-dressed. It was Sydney and stranger things had happened, she supposed. There was probably a shop open down near the quay where she could buy a new dress.

A little black hatchback pulled up. 'Get in, Elena,' said a male voice.

Thank God one of the coven had come to help her. On autopilot, she jumped in, desperate to escape her heartbreak, her embarrassment.

The car lurched forward. She turned to thank her rescuer. 'You!'

CHAPTER FIFTEEN

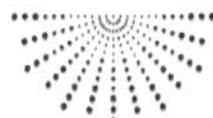

Jake Royston sagged against the wall of the lift as he headed back to his floor. His mind was in turmoil; his emotional control had never been so shattered. He was adrift, he was hurting, he was wounded — pride, soul and heart. He didn't think there would be any coming back from this.

What had caused his brain meltdown? Drugs? No drug he'd ever heard of would have had him in the space he was in. Yet it was possible — a spiked drink, maybe more than one. As soon as he thought of it he discounted the idea. Drugs seemed so opposite to Elena's style of life, her beliefs. He could not believe her capable of doing that.

He had to accept that he'd loved and lost. The loving had been golden. Now there was nothing but black-tinged grime in his heart. Was it a spell, like she kept saying? Or was it that her spell over him had shattered, shattered in time to save him from killing himself?

He'd never let a woman into his heart. He'd let her, and she had massacred it. What a fool he'd been. The delicious sexual encounters he remembered in great detail — the lovely shape of her mouth, the dimple and the wide green eyes. Her sorrow and joy on finding her father was part of his make-up now. What did it all mean? It was real, the encounter, the feelings of love.

He let himself into his office and stopped by the door. There were her sandals. He frowned as he picked them up. She must have been looking for him. He stood contemplating her shoes, trying to repress the memory of seeing her wearing them.

She had no security pass so she must have snuck in up the stairwell. Didn't that mean she cared? It was too confusing. How was he to make sense of it all? He'd let her go, too, dressed in nothing but his jacket and t-shirt. What an ass he was. Yet she was so curled up in this dark grime coating his insides that he couldn't see clearly. He hated the confusion, the un-certainty. He launched himself at the window and scanned the street below. No sign of her. She was gone.

There was nothing he could do now. Closing his eyes, he rested his head on the windowpane. It was too much. He couldn't deal with it. The only thing he could do was forget the turmoil inside. He was in his office, his work surrounding him. It would help, burying himself in casework until he could face things.

The office computer hummed to life as he pow-ered it up. There was a pile of files on his desk, left there by Pen in anticipation of his return. Shaking his head, he took a seat. Work would see him through this.

As soon as he opened his mail application, there was a list of messages from Pen. His assistant was thorough, and he'd missed a lot. He checked the time stamps and saw she'd been working that morning to catch up with the disaster his disappearance had caused.

Yet her tone was mild, not even sarcastic. He blew out a breath and sat back in his chair. Pen put up with a lot from him. He ought to give her a raise. Darn. He opened the payroll system and put it in place straight away. He added a bonus too. That should show her that he didn't take her for granted.

His head was slumped on the desk near one arm. He'd fallen asleep on the O'Reilly file. Blurry eyed, he stood up and stretched, and went to peer out to the harbor. Even at this time it was active. The lights of the passenger ship glimmered on the water, the red light atop the harbor bridge winked, even the brightly lit, smiling face of Luna Park across the other shore mocked him.

He switched on his coffee machine, and inhaled the aroma of the roasted beans while he watched the dark liquid drip into his cup. When he tested it, the ache was still there, and so was the need to cry. What had that woman done to him?

He punched the wall and then sucked on his bruised knuckles. His anger was directed at himself. How could he have let her get to him? He had managed to avoid heart entanglements before. Soft, that was it. He was getting soft. He recalled his impulsive pay rise and grinned. Definitely soft, but he didn't mind it so much. It was the ache inside of him, the gnawing empty space where she had been that bothered him more. He took the cup, sipped the hot coffee and shook his head.

Bewitched, bespelled. What did it matter? It was all over now. She didn't care about him. She'd made that clear. The look on her face that morning. The way she'd avoided eye contact, physical contact. The stiff way she'd walked out the door. Rejection was written in every line of her posture.

Back at his desk, he opened another file. Pen would be surprised that he'd caught up, given he'd been out on a sexual binge. Right, like she was going to let him get away with that without comment. Sure. Her emails may have been mild, but in person he was going to cop a roasting.

With heavy eyes, he called up his notes and wrote the required emails to get some action happening on his top corporate deal. While he thought of it, he sent off Grace Riordon's proposal to his client. He'd read the proposal in the email Elena had given him at the hotel, and he'd talked to Grace about it. The deal made sense, and the sooner he closed that chapter on his life the better. Thinking of Grace brought up memories of Elena. *Stop it.*

❀

'Why you low-down creep.'

Drew grinned at her and snapped the handcuffs over her wrists. She yelped. 'What are you doing? Take these off right now.'

'Sorry, honey, but now I know you aren't a cold-hearted bitch. I saw you melt when Royston put his mouth on you. I know what you are made of.'

Appalled, she gaped at him and then narrowed her eyes. She was right; he had been spying on her. She had to get wards straight away. Never did she think someone would be so low as to set her up and then spy on her. She wanted to throw up. What an invasion of her privacy. 'You're totally sick, you know that? I'm never going to melt for you.' She mimicked retching so he didn't mistake her meaning. 'Besides being repulsive, you're my brother.'

Drew nodded, but she could tell he still didn't believe her. He ran his hand up along her thigh. She tried to shake him off but he grasped her flesh, hard. Feelings of nausea grew and she nearly threw up for real. He must have noticed because he removed his hand.

Her heart thumped. She'd barely recovered from the Jake incident when Drew had snagged her. 'Listen. Drop me somewhere, please. You have nothing to prove. We can get DNA testing. That should give you the evidence you need.'

Shaking his head, he took a hard turn, swinging her body into his. 'No, honey. I don't need any human lies to add to the others. We're destined to be together. The coven has been linking us all year. You are the best suited to be my mate, be the mother of my children.

'So you didn't like me when we went on that date. There were too many distractions there. You have passion inside of you, real sexual feeling. You will be that way with me when we're alone. I have a place all ready for you. You won't be leaving until you have my kid inside you.'

Elena's head fell back against the headrest. He really had issues. 'You can't be serious. You want to rape me? I'm not willing, and that in human law, and ours, is a crime. You'll be driven out of the coven.'

Surely he'd not be able to go through with it. The brother-sister thing would prevent it. That calmed her a little. Unless, of course, Rory wasn't his father. No, she thought, he was. Drew had tried to kiss her before, and the revulsion had been real and powerful. He had experienced it too, but ignored it.

Drew glanced at her, his sneer evident. 'I'm already an outsider. What do I care? I want what's mine, and you're mine. I don't care that you love Royston. You had your fun. But he's not getting what's mine.' His hands gripped the steering wheel and spittle flew out of his mouth. 'He's not going to stand beside you in the coven and be the father of your children.' At a red light, he turned to face her. 'You proved you had it in you to be hot as hot. You'll be like that for me. Don't you worry. I bet you'll like being tied up. It'll turn you on.'

The light changed and he sped up.

A frustrated groan leaked out of her mouth. 'You can't do this. I promise you we are kin. It's not that I don't like you. It is something deeper than that.'

He chuckled and drove into a warehouse, stopping to get out of the car and draw the huge door shut, and plunging the place into darkness. She panicked. *Grace, help!* She sent a broadcast hail, hoping her cousin was close enough but doubting it. Their range had always been limited, and as far as she knew, Grace was on the other side of the harbor.

Drew wagged his finger at her when he got back in the car. 'Naughty, naughty. You should have done that before we came in here. I've put a blanking spell on this place. You can't call for help.'

At least he didn't know the true limits of her talents. They were very tiny. 'Drew, please. Listen to me. Call your father. Talk to him.'

He nudged the little hatchback deeper into the warehouse and stopped. 'No.' He climbed out of the car. He started hauling on a chain that was suspended by a large metal hook attached to a rafter above. Was he going to hang her from that?

Opening the passenger-side door, he grabbed the chain linking the handcuffs and pulled her out of the car. She ducked her head and stumbled.

Clinging to his shirt, she clenched her fingers and shook him. 'Look at the charm around my neck. He made it. You should be able to tell. Please, look.'

He peeled her hands from his shirt and nudged her back. She still hadn't found her feet. After steadying her, he slowly undid the buttons on Jake's jacket, pulling it apart. She shuffled away but he reached for the top of the t-shirt and ripped it, exposing her breasts. His gaze lingered there and then he lifted his hands, tweaking her nipples as he went to lift the charm. He leaned in. 'Not very good workmanship.'

As a pacifist by nature, she didn't want to hurt him. But she seized the opportunity. She drew her hands around to the side and swung hard, hitting him in the side of the head. He was taken by surprise. Although stunned, he recovered quickly, lunging at her and toppling her to the grease-stained concrete floor before she'd run more than five steps.

Hysteria overwhelmed her. She screamed as she tried to fight him off. Fear and loathing mixed together inside of her. He grabbed her hair and tried to kiss her. His lips pressed against hers, his hips grinding into her and then he paused.

He lifted his head back, puzzlement apparent in his raised eyebrows and wide, shocked eyes. Then it hit him: the revulsion, the nausea. He leaped off her and staggered a few steps before falling to his knees to vomit into a pile of scrunched up newspaper.

Crying, Elena rolled to her side, trying to regain her feet. The nausea was affecting her too, dulling her senses. She needed to get clear of the building, needed to call for help. She'd send a general call. Someone in the coven must hear; someone had to be near enough.

Drew was not sane. It had to be that. At least the

immediate danger of rape had passed. It would take a very strong warlock to control that familial repulsion. It was an age-old spell that had seeped into all of the folk. It had been cast a long time ago to stop the concentration of bloodlines and the accumulation of too much power, to stop the madness inbreeding caused.

Even though Drew couldn't ignore the repulsion of their kinship, he could still hurt her though, tie her up and humiliate her.

'Take me home now, Drew.'

He wiped his mouth with the back of his hand and nodded. 'I feel so ill.'

'Tell me about it,' Elena replied. It looked like she had broken through. He didn't look angry anymore. Instead, he was flushed, and avoided eye contact.

'I didn't believe in the spell — that it was created, and that it still existed. I thought Dad was trying to let me down easy. He was all for it, you know, before he discovered you were his. He thought a relationship and parenthood would cure me of my tendencies.'

'Tendencies?'

Subdued, he tugged the jacket over her shoulders and did up the buttons without saying a word. He unlocked the cuffs and tossed them aside, and held the car door for her so she could climb in.

'I don't like the rules much. I have a darkness in me. I know it's there. I want to explore it. Dad's been trying to divert my attention. It hasn't worked.'

'Darkness? I don't understand what you mean?' She did up her seatbelt.

He nodded as he gunned the engine. 'Probably you don't. We don't all agree with this coven's views of light and happiness, the unnatural limits on our power. We could be a powerful people if we exploited the resources around us.'

Elena's skin chilled as they exited the warehouse into the sunlight. 'You mean black magic, blood magic and death rites?' Those rites had been forbidden for more than a thousand years, and long abandoned by the folk in general.

Joining the traffic, he said. 'Yes, I want to experiment. I want to explore my potential.'

She hugged herself, feeling cold seep into her heart. It had been a very long time since the coven lost someone to the dark arts.

Drew frowned. 'Come on, sis. It's not that bad. You're safe with me. I'll get you home.'

'Please don't dabble in that stuff. You'll find a place in the coven. Maybe you could find a human partner if there are no witches here. Or what about another coven?'

'Another coven? Yes, maybe I'll try that. There is one up north.' He lapsed into silence for the rest of the journey.

Elena relaxed, easing back into her seat now that Drew seemed to be acting reasonably.

It was nearly an hour before she reached her door. 'Thanks for getting me home. I'm afraid the council were brought into this. One of them will contact you to hear your evidence."'

His dark eyes flashed. 'Why should I submit to them? I've done nothing I'm sorry for.'

'But you have done wrong.'

Drew slapped his hand on the steering wheel, his eyes narrowed when he turned back to her. 'You enjoyed it. So did Royston, until you rejected him. I still don't get why you did that.'

A surge of anger hit her, and Elena growled at him. 'You nearly caused a man's death today. You kidnapped me, and who knows what else. You should face your punishment like a man and then take your place in the coven.'

'Life's that simple for you, isn't it? Do as you are told and everything will work out. Well, not for me. There are others who don't adhere to the rules. I'm going north to find them. So long.'

With her knees shaking, Elena climbed out of the car. She spotted a neighbour and nodded. She ground her teeth. Drew made her sound like a goodie-two-shoes schoolgirl. What others was he talking about?

Drew leaned over and shut the passenger door and then sped off, his screeching tires alerting all her neighbors to her arrival. She turned to her house, hugging Jake's coat to herself to shore up her dignity. Her life used to be simple. Now, it would never be the same.

CHAPTER SIXTEEN

The act of entering her house triggered sadness. It was full of memories of Jake. Elena eased out of his jacket, catching her breath when she caught another whiff of his scent. Without glancing into the spare room, she went to the bathroom to take a shower. Dropping her panties, she climbed in and let the water wash over her. She stood there doing nothing, hoping the water would wash it all away. It was nearly ten minutes before she realized it wasn't going to be that easy, and grabbed her shower gel and started to scrub herself down.

The moment Elvira arrived, magic rippled across her skin. That woman had presence. So finally the aunt shows up, and all Elena had to show for her efforts was a big disaster.

She dried off, trying to delay the inevitable. While she wanted to talk to her aunt, it wasn't going to be easy.

Slipping on her robe, she stepped out into the living room. Aunt Elvira stood by the sofa, appearing to be checking out the paintwork on the ceiling. She was caressing Fel's neck absently as the cat draped itself over her arm. Her cat looked at Elena and blinked. She was still pretending to be real. Fel thought, *Where is your nice tom? Lost him already?* Elena wanted to howl at her in reply.

The aunt was oblivious to the exchange. Fel always had a way of being a nuisance but not advertising it.

'Hello Aunt.'

Aunt Elvira smiled, and put Fel down. The cat sauntered off to the spare room, its tail high and cheekily wagging. Elvira gestured to the parting cat. 'She's having a mood, I take it? Pretending to be a live cat.'

'Is that what you call it — a mood? I didn't even know she could do that.'

She returned her gaze to Elvira. Her aunt was a tall and plump, but very attractive. Even without her numerous and powerful talents, she was a formidable woman.

'How is Grace?'

The older woman smiled, her gaze doting when thinking of her daughter. 'Grace is doing very well, dear.' Aunt Elvira approached, and, placing her hands on Elena's shoulders, gave her a peck on both cheeks.

'We need to talk. Do sit down.'

Nervousness overcame her all of a sudden. 'Can I get you something? Wine, coffee?'

'No, dear. I don't want anything to drink. Sit.'

Hastily, Elena sat down. One did not argue when Elvira used that tone of voice.

'I've spoken to Penderton,' her aunt said as she strode around the room, bristling with nervous tension. Her fists were clenched and her shoulders tense. This wasn't a good sign.

'Which one?'

Aunt Elvira's eyebrows drew together. She took

her time answering. 'The father.' There was a slight hesitation before she finished with, 'Your father, apparently.'

'So he told you. Then you didn't know, didn't suspect?'

Elvira plonked herself down next to her on the sofa. It was then Elena could see that Elvira was just holding it together. Her cheeks were flushed, and there were signs that she'd been crying, something Elena had never seen her do. The news that Penderton was her father had shaken her deeply.

'No. I wasn't lying to you when I said your father was human.' Elena passed her a tissue when Elvira's voice cracked. 'It's what we all thought.' She paused as the tears got the better of her. Elena stroked her back.

Gaining some control, Elvira turned her reddened eyes Elena's way. 'I see that I have wronged you in many ways. Being supposedly half-human, you only had some talent when I found you. I thought that was all you would have, so I didn't put the effort into developing you.'

The tears of remorse overcame Elvira's control. Elena handed her more tissues. Her aunt blew her nose and made eye contact again. 'I was wrong. Forgive me. Rory made me see that you have potential. We must put effort into developing you. You could do so much more than make health charms.'

'Really?' Elena's heart fluttered.

'We're going to commission tutorials for you to make up for what you have missed. It will require hard work from you.'

'I have talent! Do you mean, like Grace?'

'Yes.' Elvira smiled through her tears. 'With work, you'll grow. We all keep learning, you know. I did not always have the talent that I have now. I wasn't able to teleport until I was 30. The talent is something that grows within us. Rory said he knew straight away what yours was.'

'Really? But we met only briefly.'

'Yes, you have the power to make people feel good, both in body and in spirit. That makes sense, when you think about the charms you make.'

A shiver of excitement made her leap out of her seat. 'I can be more than I am now? That is glorious news. I never thought — '

Elvira grasped her hand and squeezed lightly. 'Now, about this encounter with the lawyer...'

'Wait.' Elena closed her eyes. 'Before we go there, what happened with you and Rory? It involves my mother, obviously. Will you tell me?'

Elvira leaned back and closed her eyes. 'Perhaps I will take that drink after all. Something stronger than wine, if you have it.'

Elena went to the kitchen and looked in the cupboards. She had a small bottle of single malt whisky. That ought to do.

She grabbed some ice and sloshed the golden liquid into the glass. Her hands shook, but booze wasn't going to help settle her down. Jake Royston had left an indelible mark on her heart, and Drew had scared her. It was natural to feel shaky and hollow.

Elvira took the glass and swallowed one big mouthful, then another. Elena tucked her legs up underneath her when she took her place on the sofa and waited. Elvira glanced at her and then started to talk, staring into space as her memories unfolded. 'Not that long ago, pairings were arranged between members of the coven. Rory was to be mine. For me it was no hardship. I'd loved Rory Penderton since I was about fourteen years old. Pris was two years older than me and had refused to mate with our parents' chosen one. Actually, it was more than that. She hated the rules the coven imposed on us. Rebelled at every opportunity.'

'I'm so sorry it didn't work out with you and my father.'

Elvira sniffed and searched for a handkerchief. Elena passed her the tissues again. 'You could have been my daughter, the daughter I could have had.' She wiped her nose. 'I have Grace. I'm grateful for that, but finding out today that you were Rory's, well, it has moved me deeply.'

'I'm grateful you found me, aunt. I always have been. I love you more than I ever could a mother I have never known.'

'Part of Pris's rebellion was to stop me being with Rory. She seduced him. He denies it, takes all the blame on himself, but I knew. I saw what she did because I followed her. I didn't confront them then, but later. My mistake. I waited until Rory was too far in to extricate himself with honor. It was a real mess. Lots of angry words, lots of tears and shame.

'You see, your mother didn't know I really loved Rory. It was my secret. Stupidly, I thought if anyone knew then something would happen to prevent our joining. I was so young then. Pris hadn't loved a man — couldn't understand. To her, Rory was a means to an end. But when she looked at me, at my distress, she understood the depth of my feelings.'

'That must have been terrible for you both.'

'It was. I never saw her again. She ran away. I could never bring myself to forgive Rory. He'd fallen for Pris too, loved her. I couldn't forgive him for loving her instead of me.'

'And now how do you feel?'

Elvira's eyes widened. 'I don't really know. I feel

confused and troubled. I don't know how to make things right. I have wronged your father for so many years. The negative feelings I had damaged myself, as well as him.'

Elena told her what had happened with Drew, and his plan to rape her. She fixed another whisky for Elvira and made one for herself. 'Tell me about Drew's mother. I got the sense that there was trouble with her, too.'

'Louisa Devereau. Mad Louisa they called her. She wasn't mad, though, just scheming. You'd think Rory Penderton would have grown a bit of backbone by that time. No, she seduced him while he was still getting over Pris and me. He did care for me, I know now. Before he was a month into the relationship, she was pregnant. She demanded and received a big financial settlement, and then took off to Europe before Drew was even out of diapers. By then, Rory Penderton was over women, according to general report. I never spoke to him or saw him again until this afternoon.'

'Oh, Aunt.' Elena opened her arms and embraced Elvira. She couldn't help the tears. *So much pain.* 'So no one knows where Mother went?'

'No, only hints.'

'Hints?'

'Yes, I shouldn't tell you this because it's only rumor. There has been talk of a dark witch operating in the north.'

Elena pulled out of her aunt's embrace. 'You think my mother is this legendary dark witch?' She burst out laughing. 'Of course my mother isn't evil. She can't be. I'm not evil.'

'You see, I shouldn't have said anything. It's only a tale.' Elvira patted her on the knee. 'Forget I said it.'

Elena looked down at her hands. She was gripping them together, and so she slowly released them. 'I will forget it.' But the damage was done. The image of her mother that she had created and cherished cracked. There was no denying it.

'Now before you change the subject again, tell me how you are. Grace says you are in love with this human lawyer. Rory seemed to think so, too.'

Elena frowned. Why was everyone talking about her feelings? 'Grace talks too much. What does my father know? He's only met me once.'

Elvira smiled at her. 'Your keenness to avoid the topic is a sure sign that they are right.'

Elena squinted at her. 'But why are you pushing this? I thought you'd be against it. He's human, you know. Human, through and through. Wouldn't such a union be objectionable?'

'Not if he was the one for you. I was wrong to encourage Drew because he was a warlock. I didn't take into account his personality or anything. I was blinded by my own prejudice.'

'So, me being a full witch doesn't have anything to do with this change of heart?'

Elvira sniffed. 'You have so little faith in me...but yes, that does make things a little easier. Rory reminded me that you should be allowed to pursue your heart, regardless of who the person is.'

Elena stood up and went to put the kettle on.

'Elena?' Her aunt got up to join her.

'What is it?'

'I don't know how I feel about anything. There is no future with Jake. You should have seen him, the look on his face when the spell was lifted. He was angry and full of hate. It was a silly dream to think... to allow myself to...'

She wiped at her tears and poured hot water into cups for tea.

Elvira was quiet as she took the tea from Elena. 'I'm sorry to have such a sad face,' Elena said as she turned to make her own cup.

Elvira wiped a tear from her eye, smudging her mascara. 'I feel for you, dear. I too have loved and lost. I would spare you that pain if I could. I'm sorry I wasn't here for you.'

'Here I was thinking I did such a good job of handling things on my own.' She managed to smile through her tears.

'I have to go now,' Aunt Elvira said after a few minutes. 'Something has come up. Before I go, I forgot to mention the council have met out of session. There should be an email waiting.'

In the space of a breath, her aunt was gone, leaving her still steaming cup of tea on the bench.

CHAPTER SEVENTEEN

Before going to bed, Elena checked her email. There was a message from the council. She skimmed all the technical stuff and reached the judgement proper. They had decided that she did no wrong. That she had acted with the best intentions, and there were extenuating circumstances that needed to be considered as well. What extenuating circumstances? That she had no willpower? That she was attracted to Jake? That didn't seem right.

She logged off the computer and was about to go to bed when she remembered. Wards. She needed to place wards. That required a bit of study, so she went to the spare room, climbed up on a chair and took down the box of books she had stashed up there. Fel meowed at her, and asked what she was doing.

I'm going to study, she thought back at her cat.

Now you want to study? The cat shrugged, or gave a good impression of doing so. *You never studied when you were younger.*

Funny. I studied.

The cat faced her and flicked its tail. *You need to get that tom back...and soon.*

Thanks for the advice. For the moment I want to keep prying lowlifes out of my life.

Fel started licking her paws, then yawned. *The tom was good for you.*

Elena ignored Fel. She was not going to spill her heart to a ghost cat.

The cat, realizing that Elena wasn't leaving the room, jumped down. *I'm going to talk to the neighbors.*

Elena shrugged, watching as Fel slinked away. She turned her attention to the box of books, lifting them out one by one and spreading them on the floor. These books were what she had of Grace's special schoolbooks from the magic school, that Elena had never attended. Grace had given them to her when she moved in with Declan, thinking that Elena would find them useful. Elena had thought it was because she couldn't bring herself to throw them out.

It took a few finger glides of the indexes of five of the books to find what she was looking for. She opened the book and studied the page. There were many types of wards. The simplest she could do. Thinking on her aunt's words, she studied a more complex one. If she had the talent but hadn't developed it then she could do this one if she chose to push herself.

She was still digesting the fact that she could develop further as a witch. She'd always been happy with her lot in life, accepting things as they were. Now after Jake she wasn't. She couldn't blame her aunt for her lack of development, either. If she had wanted to, she could have pushed herself to develop as far as possible, could have been more adventurous.

Shaking her head as she read, she thought back over her life as a witch. Always caught up in being a half-witch, a discarded child and feeling sorry for herself, she had accepted that she'd always be an outsider.

She had thought herself above the folk, because she was half-human and understood that world. A sad laugh bubbled up inside her when she recollected her morally superior attitude. Must defend the humans. Must have moral fiber and not abuse the power. Where did that go when she had Jake at her mercy?

So much for being morally upright. She'd stuffed that up, hadn't she? Jake hated her now, deservedly hated her for what she'd done. She'd have to eat humble pie with him. There was no way she could leave the situation as it was. They would have to meet again, and she would have to explain herself. It was the only way she could feel right with the world.

So the council didn't lay the blame on her. That didn't cut it. Meeting with him wouldn't be in the expectation of a change of heart, but she owed it to him and to herself to make it right. She didn't want to end up like Aunt Elvira and have a tangled lump of hurt in her past, nor did she want to leave Jake damaged.

Her attention returned to the book and the ward. It was rather complicated. It took a while for her to remember the steps. After committing the spell to memory, she thought she was ready.

Climbing to her feet, she went outside to set the exterior ward. After three attempts and a lot of cussing, she was ready to give up. She peered around, hoping the neighbors weren't being disturbed by her futile efforts. She closed her eyes and calmed herself. *You can do this. You can.*

The next time she tried the ward, it slid into place like pieces of a jigsaw. With a swell of pride, she studied it. No way was another warlock or witch going to spy on her, and no way was one coming anywhere near her without her knowledge. The thought, that Drew had watched her with Jake, mortified and sickened her.

To complete the ward, she needed to place the remainder of the spell inside the house. This would allow her to monitor and control it.

Standing in the living room with her hands on her hips, she surveyed the ward with a smile of satisfaction. It was done. The most complex spell she had ever attempted. She would thank her aunt tomorrow for helping her see the way. Now that the ward was in place, she only had to maintain it to keep it working.

Turning around, a wave of tiredness hit her. Learning and setting the ward had taken hours, and the use of magic had drained her. It was three a.m. by the time she went to bed. She was so tired she didn't change the sheets. These were the bedclothes she'd shared with Jake. She inhaled deeply, drawing in his scent, despite the memories it invoked.

Elena wanted to sleep. Her feet hurt. That pain echoed her misery. A tear slid across her cheek. More followed, and before long she was sobbing and hugging a pillow. In the dark small hours, the sadness left her and she was able to contemplate the positives of her situation. A small smile broke, followed by a sniff. Some good had come of this. She'd found a father, and maybe he would find contentment. She suspected that her aunt still loved Rory Penderton, and would be able to forgive him. That would be interesting to watch.

As she lay in bed, her cat jumped up, kneaded the bed covers and lay down beside her.

Dream, Fel thought at her, and her contented purr sent Elena off to sleep.

Jake's scent filled her dreams. He smelt so good.

All through the remainder of the night she thought of him, reliving their moments together. Now, as she dreamed, she was untroubled. She saw the encounter as it should have been; free from guilt.

Fel meowed in her dreams. Mellow relaxation enveloped her. She was happy to dream of Jake and herself together again, reliving that amazing first encounter with the chin-up bar. That man had melted her. She turned over and got a mouth full of cat fur. Fel's purr didn't skip a beat, and once again she dived into her erotic dream.

Jake woke to the sound of the phone ringing. He shook his head, trying to dislodge sleep and ease the crick in his neck. He'd fallen asleep on his desk again. He blinked to clear his vision. It was overcast outside, and grey light spilled in through the windows. Sydney Harbor was washed out and sad, exactly how he was feeling.

The phone kept up its persistent wail. He lunged for it. 'Yes?'

'Hello, my name is Rory Penderton…'

Jake got ready to hang up the phone. Damn telemarketing at this time of the morning. He clenched his jaw, ready to slam the phone down and then paused. That name was familiar. He brought the handset back to his ear. 'Penderton?'

'Yes, we met at my house on Saturday.'

Klaxons were going off in his brain. He was trying not to think about her. 'Yes, you're Elena's father.'

'Yes, I am. I need to talk to you.'

'Sure, anytime,' he replied. Maybe when it didn't hurt so much and in a situation he could control.

'Excellent. May I come up?'

Jake nearly dropped the phone. 'You're at my building? Now?'

'Yes, just outside.'

Jake checked his watch. It was 6.30 a.m. on Monday morning. He'd have to let him in.

'I'll come down.'

Within five minutes, Rory Penderton was in Jake's office. Jake rested his rear on the front of the desk, and folded his arms across his chest. He kept his face impassive as he took in the older man standing in front of him. Elena sending her father was an interesting ploy, one that surprised him. She must like to strike while the wound was fresh.

'Elena doesn't know I'm here.'

Jake chewed his cheek. How did Penderton know what he was thinking? Still, he didn't feel guilty thinking ill of Elena. It was good to give his anger focus.

'So, to what do I owe the honor of this visit?' Jake asked, locking his expression down. He didn't want to give anything else away. His feelings were his own, and not for others to scrutinize.

Rory Penderton sent his gaze around the room and rested for a brief moment on the view. The sun had managed to break through the cloud cover, adding a silvery glow to the atmosphere.

'No honor is intended. I think we need to talk about things, about who you are.'

This got Jake standing up straight. It certainly wasn't what he was expecting the conversation to be about. No pleas for forgiveness on Elena's behalf. No mention of her at all.

'Is this some kind of joke? Because it's not funny.'

Rory Penderton relaxed his stance, but his gaze was fierce. 'Is your grandfather Gregor Royston?'

Jake rocked back on his heels. It was certainly

being dished up to him today and it wasn't even seven a.m. 'Yes. I've never met him though. You have a problem with him?'

Rory shook his head. 'No, son. You need to go visit him. I've come to take you.'

Jake laughed, a bitter chuckle. 'Why would I do that? I don't know the old bastard.'

The older man opposite him shrugged. 'You will get to know him.'

Jake was concerned that Elena's father was serious. 'My father hated him. I don't even get on with my father very well. If they're alike, I wouldn't even waste my time.'

Rory stared, his grey-green eyes piercing. Jake shook himself. That was uncanny, because he was sure he sensed Penderton looking into him. Yet, the older man kept on staring. Jake squirmed a little and moved behind his desk to break eye contact.

'You'd better leave. I've got a busy day ahead. In fact, I have a busy life, so don't bother contacting me again.'

Penderton didn't budge. Not that he expected that he would. He'd shown a bit of bluster, but he may as well be lying on the ground waiting to get his stomach scratched for all the effect he had on Elena's father.

'Jake you need to do this. It's important.' There was no hint of desperation in Penderton's voice. He stood firm, like he'd never back down. He detected hints of Elena in him. Oh God, Elena. She'd turned his life upside down, and now her relatives were giving him grief.

Jake sat down and leaned back in his chair. 'I don't need to do anything. You should leave.'

Rory stepped forward, grabbing the chair in front of him as if he owned the place and sat down. Before

Jake could react, the old man leaned forward and said, 'It won't take much of your time. I can guarantee you won't regret it.'

A laugh escaped. It was like spam, click this link and you can collect your lottery winnings. 'Is he dying? Am I to inherit or something? I'm not interested. I've got stacks of money. I don't need to see some old man who has never been interested in me.'

Rory sat back in his chair and folded his arms. 'That bad, huh?'

Jake sent him a scathing look and pursed his lips. He didn't trust himself to respond. It might all come out — the black grime of rejection, the loss, the pain.

'I know you're hurting. I can sense it from where I'm sitting.'

Jake jerked once, unable to stifle his reaction. His mouthed an 'o' of surprise, and let out a squeak.

The old man kept talking though, not even interested in his response. 'I don't know if the old man is dying. I expect not, he's as strong as an ox. I don't know if he's as rich as a sultan, or as poor as a church mouse. We're not on such terms. But I do know where he is, and you need to go see him.'

'Why?' Jake hated how plaintive his voice sounded. He was intrigued by this man, and yet also keen to be free of him.

'For Elena's sake.'

'Ah, I thought we'd come down to her.' The mention of Elena sent emotions charging through his body, blending with the hurt, making it fresh as the moment it was inflicted. 'Why should I care about her?'

'Because you're in love. It's killing you right now.'

'Stop! Stop with this voodoo thing of reading me. I am not in love with her. Ask any woman who knows me. It's impossible. I don't fall in love with women, particularly ones that don't want me.'

Rory shook his head. 'This will help, believe me.'

'You're nuts.' Jake threw up his hands. What did he have to do to get rid of this guy?

Rory shrugged. 'Maybe I am. It's not infectious, by the way, being nuts, I mean. I'll tell you this. Once, long ago, I didn't do something. I didn't say the words I should have said. I suffered. I made another person suffer. The ramifications kept on spreading. I don't want that for you. I certainly don't want that for Elena.'

Jake stood up, sending his chair rocking back. He leaned forward, his fists resting on the tabletop. 'Look, old man. No offense, but I'm not in love with your daughter. I don't give a shit about whether she suffers or not. She probably deserves it.' He was speaking lies, yet he was too stubborn to admit it to Elena's father, even if he acknowledged it himself.

Penderton didn't even flinch at Jake's aggressive posturing. He rubbed his chin as he looked Jake up-and-down with a slight smile. 'Have it your way, son. Call me if you change your mind.'

He tossed his card on the desk as he stood, and then he left.

Jake was so conflicted. What did he have to lose? What was he afraid of? It was his grandfather, someone he'd never met but had always been curious about. Switches in his brain clicked, and he was moving.

Jake caught Penderton as he was pushing the glass door of the office open. 'Wait. You're right. It can't hurt to go with you. I've got nothing to lose, except another day's work.'

Rory held the door open. 'Come on then, son.

What are you waiting for? I've been dying to have a ride in that flash car of yours.'

Jake checked his pockets for his keys and grinned. 'In that case, you're in for a treat. Wait two minutes.'

Jake left a scribbled note for Pen to let her know not to worry.

❧

Dead to the world, when the phone rang Elena sprang from the bed with a cry of surprise on her lips. Rubbing sleep from her face, she groped for the phone which blared impatiently at her. Looking at the display, she noted it wasn't a number she knew. Sitting on the edge of the bed, she answered, 'Yes.'

She eyed the clock. It was 10.30 a.m. She'd overslept. 'Hello, this is Penelope Matthews, Jake's executive assistant. We met briefly the other day.'

Her heart thumped. Was he wanting to see her? 'Oh yes, I remember. Good morning.'

Elena could hear the woman shuffling papers. 'I was wondering if Jake was with you. He's been into the office but he's not here now.'

Elena swallowed her disappointment. 'I'm sorry. He's not with me. I don't know where he is.'

There was silence for a few moments. 'Thank you. Sorry for troubling you, Miss Denholm.'

'No, that's fine. You aren't disturbing me.'

'Wait…can you tell me…is everything okay…you know…between you two?'

Elena wanted to pretend she didn't know what the woman was asking, but couldn't.

'We had a bit of a misunderstanding. Have you seen him?'

The other woman let out a sigh. 'No, not at all. But he worked all night. I can tell from the emails and the work he's done. It's not like him to pull an all-nighter. I'd better go. Hopefully we'll meet again.'

'Bye.' Elena sat on the bed and stared at the phone. Jake had worked after their encounter. Obviously, she was a problem that was easily pigeonholed or compartmentalized. That's what businesspeople did, wasn't it? Put their emotional issues aside and continued doing their work? She had not developed that facility. Her whole life was out of kilter because of what had happened between them.

Fel jumped on her, startling her out of a doze. *Is this the best you can do?*

Elena reached for her cat. *Yes.*

Her cat thought she was pathetic, a point with which she agreed. *Why are you real now?*

The cat eyed her, and tilted its head. *I found that I could. For the right tom, I'd do anything.*

Oh Fel. So would I.

Tears gathered in the corner of her eyes. Elena buried her face in her pillow. A few hours of misery in her bed were all she could stand. She had to get on with life, so she had a shower and dressed.

Coming into her living area, the first thing she saw was Jake's coat on the chair back. She picked it up and bagged it. She'd have it cleaned and then return it to him. It was the best way to talk to him again.

After picking up some groceries, she lounged around the house all day, feeling sorry for herself. Every hour or so she'd pick up one of Grace's magic books and study it. Sprawled on her bed with the book sliding out of her grasp was how Grace found her.

'Hi there,' Grace said brightly, as she tucked Elena's house key into her purse. Elena hadn't reset the ward after she came in.

'Mmmpf…hi. Go away.'

Grace sat on the bed and slapped Elena lightly on the bottom. 'Come on, up you get.'

Elena screwed her eyes shut. Grace's cheerful voice grated on her. She wanted to be left alone in her misery. 'Grace, I'm not in the mood.'

'Not in the mood for one of my hugs? Pre-posterous!'

Elena couldn't hold back the smile. How could she resist that? She was miserable, and misery loved company, so they said. She crawled into a sitting position and nodded, while dragging her bedraggled hair from her face.

Grace enveloped her in a hug. That was Elena's undoing. All the little straps that were restraining the hurt undid themselves. Elena let go of a sob then lost herself to her tears while Grace stroked her back and soothed her.

"Let it out, Elena. There's no point holding it in. You're hurting. Seeing you hurt hurts us as well.'

'Thank you,' Elena cried some more. 'It's all such a mess.'

'It surely seems that way right now. But that doesn't mean it can't be fixed. There will be sunshine in your life again.'

CHAPTER EIGHTEEN

Despite wishing otherwise, Jake found Rory Penderton a pleasant companion as they headed up past Gosford to Lake Macquarie. Thankfully the older man kept to neutral topics, like how long his family had been in Sydney and his views on the latest model BMWs compared to Audis. It was better than hearing more about the spell mumbo jumbo.

The light conversation also kept Jake's mind off things, like how much turmoil meeting his grandfather was causing him. He'd never thought it would feel like a betrayal of his own father. How easily had his father's prejudices rubbed off on him? Up until that moment, he didn't even know that they had.

A quick glance in the rear view mirror and Jake was relieved to find that he didn't resemble his father that much. The expression of disdain his father always wore was absent from his face. His father had experienced many disappointments, particularly in love, and it showed.

At Morriset, Jake turned off onto Macquarie Street, heading toward the waters of Lake Macquarie. Jake checked his rear view mirror as he merged with the traffic, slipping in ahead of a VW Combi van that chugged along the road. 'I hope you don't mind me asking, but what was the situation where you didn't say what you should have — that action you regretted not taking?'

After skimming the surface, Jake wanted to dig a little deeper. Rory Penderton had stuck his nose in Jake's business, so he felt justified in exploring the other man's life.

Rory cast him a look and bit his bottom lip. He nodded, and then started talking. 'Fair enough question. I was supposed to be with Elvira, Elena's aunt. I'd known her most of my life. I was very happy at the prospect of being her mate — you know it's like getting married. I remember being with her, how beautiful she was and how her energy was so light.

'Pris was her elder sister, more my own age. She was the opposite in personality to Elvira. She wasn't pretty, so much, but had an austere beauty, and her energy was dark and dangerous. Being with her was a bit like putting your hand in the fire, knowing you'll get burned. When Pris decided to be with me, things got complicated.'

'Don't they always?' That was a throwaway line. The only woman who'd made his life complicated was Elena. The other women in his life had never got close enough to entangle themselves.

Rory looked out the window. 'One night Pris came to see me. Materialized right in my bedroom. Did I mention she was a very powerful witch for her age?'

Jake's eyes rolled up. Rory lifted a shoulder and continued with his story. 'She was pretty full on, if you know what I mean. Sexually experienced. I wasn't. She was my first. It was intense. So intense.

'I thought I loved her because of what we'd

shared. She intoxicated me with sex, with sensation. I forgot all about my commitment to Elvira. I was only thinking of the next time I'd be with Pris, the next time she would take me to a new level of ecstasy. Yet Pris didn't really want me. It was all a tactic to her.'

Jake could understand the older man's pain. He had a similar experience with his first sexual encounter with a more experienced older woman. It was probably that along with his view of his parents' relationship that sealed his heart shut.

'And then what happened?'

Rory's voice thickened. 'Elvira caught us together. Not just together, but in the thick of it. I'll never forget the pain in her face. The betrayal I saw in her eyes. Pris, though, was shattered. She was shaking after the encounter, crying up a storm, too. She was a feisty woman, full of her own destiny but I gathered from her that Elvira was the only person she loved. She hated her parents, hated the rules. She didn't know that Elvira truly loved me. She thought Elvira was being obedient in agreeing to mate with me. That night she left Sydney, never to return.'

'So this Pris, this is Elena's mother we're speaking of, isn't it?' Rory nodded. 'Did she not say anything to you?'

'I can remember every word as if it was yesterday, but I won't repeat what she said verbatim. It was something along the lines of I was a useless fuck, that she hated every moment we were together and that she was using me to stop Elvira being with me.'

Jake swallowed. 'Ouch.' He turned into Fishery Point Rd, heading for Sugar Bay. 'So did you try to talk to Elvira again? Make things right?'

Rory's voice was even thicker. 'No. I thought about sending her a message saying I was sorry, but didn't. I never heard or spoke to her again. What could I say? I was a mess, confused, hurt, angry. Most of all, I was ashamed. I had hurt someone I cared about.

'I met Drew's mother not long after, and fell into a disastrous relationship with her. I knew I deserved it for what I'd done. I was still confused, too. It took me a few years to sort the lust from the love. I had loved Elvira. I never told her, never asked for forgiveness, never gave us a chance. For near on twenty seven years she's hated me with a vengeance.'

'That's it?'

Rory's brow furrowed as he cast another glance to Jake. 'I withdrew from the community, the coven, to keep out of her way. I watched from the distance as she had a child with Ernst Riordon. I watched her spend ten years of her life with a man she didn't love all because of my mistake.'

Jake slowed down to match the speed limit in a residential zone. 'I can see that could weigh heavily. You still love Elvira now, don't you?'

'Yes, I met with her yesterday. It was a rather emotional encounter, but she loves me, even though I don't deserve it. I don't think she has totally forgiven me yet. Finding out I was Elena's father changed everything for us both.

'We have a future together. However, there have been many years wasted, years we can't have back, children we can't make.'

Jake sucked in a breath. There was so much hope and pain in Rory's words. He tried not to think about Elena but the memory of her sweet face kept arising unbidden. 'We are nearly at Gregor's house.'

'I know. Slow down and turn right here.'

Jake's heart raced. He closed his eyes and breathed deep when he killed the engine. They'd pulled up outside a large, split-level beach house with a boat floating next to a jetty at the rear. Jake looked to the lake and was astounded by the view. It was a dream house; quiet, water, sun and a boat.

Gregor Royston came out of the front door and onto the lawn to greet them. A tingling raced all over Jake's skin, a sensation he put down to anxiety.

Jake stood stock-still after climbing out of the car. His grandfather looked a lot like him. He sensed great energy from Gregor; he looked way too young to be his grandfather, no more than late forties, yet he had to be eighty if he was a day. He looked younger than his own father did.

Their eyes met. An electric charge shot right into him. He shook himself. What was that?

Gregor stopped. 'Penderton, thank you for bringing him. Go up into the house. My grand-daughter Bethanea will fix you a drink, make you comfortable.'

Rory nodded and left them alone. Jake had only that moment to pull himself together. He put out his hand. 'I'm Jake.'

Gregor looked at his hand and then up at him. There were tears in the old man's eyes. His grandfather opened his arms and launched himself at him. 'I'm so happy to see you, son.' He grabbed Jake to him with a surprisingly strong grip. At first Jake wanted to pull away, unused to physical contact, but then he relaxed as his grandfather patted him on the back. 'Welcome, welcome. I knew about you. I'd almost given up hope of ever meeting you.'

Holding him by the shoulders, Gregor looked Jake over. 'You look like me when I was a young buck. How's your father?'

'The same.'

Gregor studied him for a minute or two and nodded, his eyes trailing down and then up. 'You're a mess. What's been going on?'

'Rory thinks I was hit by a love spell that went bad. I think he's crazy.'

Gregor laughed. 'We'll see about that. You're a mess, and it's not just the spell. You're full of knots of emotion, so tangled it's amazing you can even think. We'll have to work hard to clean you up. You'll stay, won't you? Stay a few days?'

A crevice of hope opened up inside Jake. He liked Gregor. He wanted to stay. He'd put up with the mumbo jumbo if he had to. He looked to the lake; it had been a long time since he'd been out on a boat.

Gregor led him inside, arm around his shoulder. 'Yes, we can even go out on the lake while you are here.'

Jake settled into Gregor's household. He met his cousin, Nea, a shortened version of the name Bethanea, who was a very attractive twenty one year-old, with blonde hair down to her waist, white skin and a smattering of freckles across the bridge of her nose. Her eyes were the same vivid blue as his own, a trait handed down from Gregor, he assumed. Nea bestowed a big hug on him and called him cuz.

A guest room at the back of the house on the ground floor had been given to him for his stay. It held a large bed and had its own en suite bathroom. He'd love to bring Elena here. He stopped himself at the thought. Closing his eyes, he held the bridge of his nose. Tears threatened. He couldn't keep bottling up his emotions. On the one hand, he wanted Elena, a future with her, and on the other, he couldn't bear the agony of her rejection. He couldn't shake it off.

After getting a grip on himself he opened the sliding doors to the little veranda and studied the jetty and the large cruiser moored there. A small beach curved around to join the rest of the bay. Jake left the door open so he could listen to the lake lap against the shore.

At dinner, where Gregor barbecued fish and Nea provided an array of salads, they sat around and chatted. 'Don't be shy, cuz,' she quipped as she set down a bowl of homemade aioli. 'You're among family now.'

Jake couldn't help but smile at her. Her mood was infectious. The welcome feeling that at first seemed odd was natural to him after only a few hours. It was weird. He'd had very little family life once he'd been sent to boarding school.

They sat around while eating the fresh-caught fish and chatted about the lake, the weather and family. Jake did his best to keep up with the names of people he hadn't met. He had an uncle that his father had never mentioned, Nea's dad. Gregor's wife had passed away a few years before, so Nea had moved in to keep house for him.

They finished eating dessert, a freshly made pavlova with an amazing fruit salad on the side, when the general discussion quieted. 'So Jake,' Gregor said, as he sat back to take a sip of his cider. 'How long have you known you were a warlock?'

Jake nearly choked on the beer he was drinking. 'Warlock?'

Gregor turned to Rory and lifted an eyebrow. 'He doesn't know, or doesn't believe?'

'Both,' Jake supplied.

Rory tilted his head. 'I suspected he was, but he was never going to believe me. He moved through my house with ease, the wards didn't touch him. I thought it best to bring him here. It would explain why that love spell went bad so quickly. It would ex-plain why Elena couldn't resist the attraction. His prime talent is persuasion. I bet he's been using it all his life without knowing it.'

'Look, you guys, I'm really enjoying myself here. Don't start with this spell business.'

Gregor drew his brows down and glared at him. 'Peter never told you, then?'

'Dad? Told me what?'

'Call him. Ask him why he left, ask him why he never sees me.'

Jake patted the phone in his pocket and fished it out to check the charge. He had enough juice to make the call. He'd left his charger in the office.

With a nod to the others, he left the house and took a walk along the beach. His father picked up and, probably for the first time in his life, he was honest with him.

It was difficult. His father yelled and ranted when he heard Jake was with Gregor, and got downright nasty when he caught on that Jake might have talent. 'It's his fault. He married a human,' Peter said derisively. 'I don't want anything to do with them, or you, if you stay with them.'

Jake hung up and shook his head. Could he believe? His father believed it, and was bitter about not having any of the talent and jealous of Jake's potential. Rory had said his talent was persuasion. As he looked back on his life, he realized that was right. He could persuade people, particularly when they were in the room with him.

It was around midnight by the time Jake was ready to face Gregor. The turmoil he'd experienced earlier was easing, but he was unwilling to stride into this new life. The mental adjustment didn't come easily. He thought having an extended family was pretty out there, but a magical family, and him a warlock?

Well, he might need a few more beers before that made any sense.

Gregor was waiting for him when he came back to the house. 'It's not all bad, son. Your father didn't have any talent. He hated that. Now if you take a seat, we'll start on cleaning up that spell.'

Jake nodded numbly and sat on the deckchair. Gregor wasn't going to hurt him, he was pretty certain of that, and insanity wasn't contagious. 'Look at the moon to keep you occupied. Talk to me if you feel strange.'

The waxing crescent moon rode scudding clouds. From nowhere, he sensed heat in his body. It was as if someone was strumming their hot fingers across the surface of his mind. He experienced tugs, and then was suddenly lighter in those spaces. Each time he commented, Gregor's voice soothed him.

He was still in the chair when the sun rose over the lake. Gregor sat with his head in his hands. 'That's enough for now. You have been through shit, Jake. I can see why the spell fractured like that, leaving sticky grime clinging to you. We'll need a few more sessions before you start feeling right.'

'What do you mean?' Jake was exhausted but he was also afraid that someone had seen into the lonely boy he had been.

'He loved you, but he was never good at showing it.'

Ah, Jake thought. *He did see into me.* He swallowed and then lifted his head to meet Gregor's gaze. 'I don't believe he does. Even last night he was full of anger and jealousy.'

Gregor nodded wearily, and slapped him on the knee. 'Rest now. This afternoon we'll go out on the lake, and see what else we can do about your inner landscape. There's years of gunk layered in there.'

Jake did go to bed. He dreamed of Elena, and those dreams were no longer tinged with despair. He was still confused by what had happened, but he no longer blamed her. Now he actually believed her about the spell, about her misgivings, about her feelings.

Now he wanted to see her again, to test out his feelings — and hers.

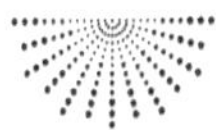

CHAPTER NINETEEN

On Thursday, Elena picked up Jake's coat from the dry cleaners with the intention of returning it to him. The past few days in her house had been long and lonely and miserable. The only highlight had been practicing some of the spells from Grace's books.

Every day, Grace came for a quick visit. Mainly, she came to bring some fresh food and provide chitchat, because Elena didn't care a hoot about her own health or mental wellbeing in the state she was in.

Elena had never been so low, and it was the pits. She should pull herself out of it, but found it hard to pick up where she had left off — before Jake.

Aunt Elvira sent invitations to take tea that Elena didn't accept. She wasn't quite up to the social thing. She wasn't angry with her aunt, but she had a lot to digest about herself, about her parentage, and about suffering in general.

It took her most of the morning to get ready. She shampooed her hair and blow-waved it so it was glossy and straight. She put on a little bit of make-up, some shadow to her eyes and some light color to her lips. The irony was that she wanted to look like she'd made an effort, but not too much of one. The state of her make-up would not be the thing that swung this for her.

Pulling out her notebook, she checked off and re-hearsed everything she wanted to say to Jake while her nail polish dried. When she thought she had that right, she contemplated her wardrobe. This only set off memories of that scene on the roof of the building where her dress blew away. Perhaps pants would be better.

Her hand passed over the green dress she'd worn the first time they'd met. Yes, that was it. She slipped it on and found a pair of strappy san-dals to go with it. At least her feet had healed. After climbing all those stairs, she'd been hardly able to walk for the next couple of days. Her healing spells and lazing around in bed had helped that.

It was sprinkling rain that greeted her as she left the house. She put up her daisy-patterned umbrella, and swung the coat hanger with the plastic cover protecting Jake's jacket over her shoulder as she headed to the wharf. Luckily, she had timed her walk so the ferry pulled up as she arrived.

Once on the ferry she took a spot close to the prow. Her eyes ate up the view of the harbor. She lis-tened to the waves, allowing the motion to soothe her nerves.

She wholeheartedly wished her stomach would stop churning. What was the worst that could hap-pen? He'd still hate her, and that was no change from now. Thinking that way was the only method to calm her mind, and accept the possible outcome of her meeting with Jake.

As long as she had managed to get what she

wanted to say off her chest, it would be a good out-come emotionally for both of them, at least.

Once she'd arrived in Circular Quay, she walked slowly toward Jake's building. Pedestrians pushed past her or cut and swerved to avoid bumping into her. It was bad manners to walk slowly in the crowd, but it was all she could do to keep herself together. Her heart beat double time. Her stomach was a pin-cushion. She stopped in the street when she caught sight of those doors and lifted her head to take in the top of the building.

Someone bumped into her, and then another person.

'Sorry,' she said, and then rejoined the flow of pedestrians. She should have known better than to stop dead still in a crowded street.

As she neared the doors, she angled herself out of the pedestrian flow and spilled into the doorway. The revolving door swallowed her and then spat her out on the other side.

The green marble flooring reminded her of the last time she'd crossed the entry foyer. She closed down those recollections and walked to the lift. The security guard gave her a curious look as she passed by, but did not request she sign a register or ask her business. There were a lot of firms sharing the build-ing. She supposed they all had their own security and reception arrangements.

The lift arrived at the thirty fifth floor. In a few steps, she would be at his office.

She hovered in the corridor, peering through the glass doors. Pen was at work, talking on the phone. When the assistant finished talking, she pushed open the doors.

Pen looked up, her mouth dropping open. 'Miss Denholm?'

'Please, call me Elena. I've come to see Jake to re-turn this.' She lifted the dry cleaning bag off her shoulder. 'Is he free?'

'He's not with you?' Pen's expression looked troubled, her eyebrows drawn low.

'No?'

'Oh dear.' Pen chewed her lip as her gaze went to the phone.

'What is it?' A sudden surge of panic hit her. What if he was still suicidal after all? What if the ordeal had been too much for him?

She tried to sort through everything. He'd worked all night after the end of the spell. She spotted a chair and sat down before she collapsed. He had to be all right. It had to be something else. Please, goddess, let it be something else.

Pen rose up from her chair and came around the desk. 'I haven't seen or heard from him all week. Re-member, I called you?'

Nausea enveloped Elena and a fine sweat broke out on her forehead. Pen took the dry cleaning bag from her limp hand and hung it up. Then she passed her a glass of water. 'Are you okay?'

Elena drank the water and took a few breaths. 'I'm fine.' She put her head forward into her hands. This was not what she was expecting. Rejection yes, yelling maybe, but no Jake? She shifted her gaze to the woman. 'Are you saying you don't know where he is?'

Pen nodded and rubbed her chin. 'You see, I didn't quite believe you when you said he wasn't with you. Jake's never taken time off work for a woman. Seeing he skipped a day or so, it only seemed natural to take more.' Her intent gaze appraised Elena. 'You're the first. I'm surprised and pleased. He's been a hard-hearted bastard…sorry…for too long now. It was nice to see that he had some heart after all, could feel some kind of attachment.'

'He did say he'd had a lot of women.'

Pen nodded. 'Huh, that's right. He didn't care much for them, other than as objects. Yet you seemed different. I thought…well…maybe I was wrong. Maybe it wasn't love at first sight at all. Oh lord, where has he got to?'

Elena reached out and touched the other woman's hand. 'Please don't worry. I'm sure he's fine. We had a misunderstanding.'

Elena could sense through the skin-on-skin contact Pen's genuine worry for Jake. Love, but not passion. 'I'm sure he'll turn up soon,' Elena said, as comfortingly as she could manage.

Pen's eyes were teary. She reached for a tissue and blew her nose. 'But it's not like him to clear out. He did a week's work in one night, and then left. He left a scribbled note to say he was going away for a few days. Security said he left with some bloke before seven a.m. Monday.'

'Young or old?' Not Drew again. Surely he wouldn't be so vindictive as to come back to kidnap Jake. But he'd kidnapped her, without a second thought or apology. There was no telling what Drew would do.

Pen shrugged. 'Sorry, I didn't ask.'

Elena collected herself and stood up. 'I'd better go.' She needed to contact Drew and make sure Jake's disappearance had nothing to do with him. Maybe Rory would be the better choice.

'Sure.' She handed Elena her folded umbrella, which she had dropped as she came in.

Pen held the door for her. 'Look,' Elena said as she paused on the threshold, 'would it be possible to let me know when he's back?'

Pen shrugged. 'If I can. He's my boss and…well… you know, if he says no…'

Elena lowered her head and stepped through the door. Pen stuck her head out. 'You know you're good for him. You lighten his spirit.'

'Sure I do.' Elena chuckled.

'No, you do. He gave me a raise and a bonus this week. I haven't had one of those in a while. He's not stingy or anything like that. He doesn't think about it.'

The lift arrived. 'Thank you. I hope you hear from him soon.'

'Yeah, me too.'

The lift doors shut. Elena leant against the rear of the elevator car, trying to stop the flow of tears. That was not what she'd been expecting. Where was Jake? Was he safe? How was she going to bear another day of this misery? She needed to tell him how she felt, even if he threw it back at her.

By the time she made it out to the street, it was pouring, hard. She hung back under the pediment of the building to wait it out. She checked her watch; there was some breathing space before the ferry home.

She needn't have bothered. She was saturated before she made the ferry, and the trip across the harbor was uncomfortable. As she was already wet, the wind managed to chill her to the bone. She supposed if her talent was better developed she could have deflected the weather like more gifted folk could do. Feeling low meant she didn't care about being wet. It suited her mood.

On entering her house, her reflection greeted her. Her hair was wet and straggly, her dress stained by rain. Washed out and pale. *Great.*

There was no answer from her father's number. A

quick call to Grace and she found no one had heard from Drew, either. It was as though he'd scampered away after his attempted abduction.

After saving her father's number in her phone, she sent him a text. *Jake's missing. I'm worried.*

Straight away, a text came in. *Jake's fine. Don't worry.*

Gaping at the phone, she leant against the breakfast bar. How did her father know about Jake?

A big sigh of relief fled out of her. She tried calling her father again, but he didn't pick up. Glaring at the phone, she tossed it on the sofa. She was still in her wet clothes and began to shiver.

'This calls for a bath,' she said to herself, and went to run one. As the water flowed in, she tossed in some bath salts, a blend she had made herself of lavender, rose geranium and jojoba. Inhaling it, the floral essences caressed her mind and her aching body.

Staring at the ceiling through the steam did little to help her mind settle. Afterwards, she stood at the door to the spare room. There were a lot of orders to fill, but her heart wasn't in it. Turning her back on her work, she went to bed for a nap. Surprisingly, she had no trouble getting off to sleep.

A few hours later, Fel leaped up onto the bed with a screech. Drowsily, she lifted her head. 'Fel what now?'

Hungry, the cat thought at her.

'You can't be; you're dead.'

The cat snuck over and licked her face. 'Oh, stop. I'm sleeping.' She put the sheet over her head. Fel settled herself on top of it. Elena dozed back off to sleep. The rain had stopped.

Some hours later there was a tickle in her mind, and then pins and needles in her feet and hands.

There was a warlock hovering on the perimeter of her ward. Bolting upright, she sent Fel flying with an indignant yowl.

Careful! That hurt.

'Sorry,' she said as she threw on some clothes and opened the front door. Under the streetlight stood Rory Penderton, her father. It was rather late but she lowered the ward and he walked up to her, put his hands on her shoulders and kissed her forehead.

'It's good to see you.'

Stepping back to let him inside, she got a sense of excitement and tension from him.

'What is it? What's going on?'

Fel slunk around his feet and he looked down. 'I heard about your cat. It looks alive, but I thought…'

'Yes, it's an undead cat, with an identity crisis.' She knelt down. 'Out you go, Fel, and find a big fat rat to nibble on.'

She eased the cat outside and shut the door, leaning against it to gaze at her father.

'So, tell me.'

He grinned. 'Make me a coffee. I'll tell you all about it.'

Her father made himself comfortable on the sofa while she faced the horrible coffee machine. Since Jake had fixed it, though, it wasn't nearly as scary as it used to be.

She carefully brought the coffee over and handed it to him. He inhaled appreciatively.

'Ah that's good. I feel like I've been in the wilderness.'

'Have you been away? With Drew?'

His expression clouded. 'Drew,' he said. 'I did see him. That's another story.'

'Well what is it? I can tell something has got you wound up.'

'I went north.'

'North?'

'Lake Macquarie, to be precise. There's a coven up there.'

Elena chewed on her bottom lip. Drew had mentioned a group in the north. She tilted her head, her expression curious.

'A while back, when I was young, there was a big division in the coven. A group left Sydney and set up a coven for themselves around the lake.'

'You told me to not to worry. Does this coven have anything to do with Jake?'

'Yes,' he replied.

'So tell me,' she said, clenching her hands.

'He came with me. I took him to the lake.'

Elena's face creased up in a frown. 'You took him to the lake? Why, for goddess sake? Do you know his assistant has been out of her mind with worry?'

'I'm sorry his people were worried. He left a note, so I thought that would be sufficient. I didn't think he'd stay so long.'

Elena's mind was reeling. Jake had spent the week with her father. Why?

'Apparently it's not normal for him to just disappear. He has a busy law practice.'

Her father shrugged. 'It was worth the worry, believe me.'

Questions tumbled over one another in her head. She didn't know where to start.

'Tell me what is going on.'

'There was a warlock named Royston among those that left our coven. Gregor Royston married a human woman. Created quite a stir by doing so. He thumbed his nose at the establishment here, and helped establish the new coven.'

'But there's no rule against marrying a human.'

'No, not now and not then. But there was pressure to keep the bloodlines pure and conserve talent. Royston was a big talent, and a lot of pressure was brought to bear. He didn't like it, not one bit. Contact was lost after that. I mean, we knew they were there, this other coven, but it was not discussed.'

'Royston...so you're saying Jake's a descendent of this warlock?'

'Yes, but that's not my story to tell.'

Elena clenched her fist until her nails dug into her palm. 'So, what can you tell me?'

'You've heard the rumors of the dark witch of the north?'

Elena nodded. 'Vaguely.'

'I met her.'

She cast her glance up and down. 'You're still whole, so I'm taking it she didn't turn you into a toad.'

Rory Penderton laughed, and then grew serious. 'She's your mother.'

Elena's eyes widened. 'My mother is the dark witch of the north? You're kidding me. Aunt Elvira tried to tell me but I laughed in her face. How is it possible that my mother is a dark witch?'

Rory lowered his gaze. 'It was good to know she was alive, at least. For years I've wondered what became of her. I thought she killed herself from remorse...'

Elena couldn't help feeling excited. Her mother had been found — the mother who had abandoned her. 'What did she say? Did she ask about me?'

Rory reached out and took her hand, his eyes darkening. 'We did talk about you. She is glad you are with Elvira. She said you were meant to be.'

'Does she want to see me?'

Rory squeezed her hand. 'No. I'm sorry, she doesn't.'

A sob caught in her throat. Her mother didn't want to see her. She guessed that made sense; the woman had abandoned her. Her father wiped the tears from her cheek. 'You really don't want to meet this woman. She is a dark witch, in every sense of the term. There is no going back for her. If she wanted to see you, I'd be afraid for you.'

Elena blinked. 'I don't understand. I can taste your excitement. I thought you had good news.'

Rory tilted his head and smiled. 'It's a great weight off my mind to know that she's alive. That I wasn't responsible for her death. That my actions didn't destroy so many lives.'

'That's not all of it.'

'Like I said, not my story to tell.'

'So did you bring Jake back?'

'No. He's still there but he'll be back soon, I'm sure.'

He hugged her to him as he polished off his coffee. 'I'd better go. Elvira is expecting me.'

Elena stood up. 'Good, good. I'm glad you two are getting along, finally.'

Pleasure exuded from her father. 'Love never dies, Elena. True love lasts. Elvira still loves me after all this time.'

Elena froze while she digested the news. Elvira was her mother in all the ways that counted. That she now loved her father, a man she hardly knew, was a bit daunting. Yet she trusted that her aunt had the right of it, particularly if her love had lasted that long.

She beamed. 'That's great. I'm so happy for you both.'

'Thank you. Elvira insists on you coming around.

No more moping about Jake. If you don't come around, she'll come and fetch you.'

Elena laughed again. 'Yes, yes. I'll turn up before then.'

'Good.' Her father turned to leave.

'Hang on, what about Drew?'

'He's gone up north and joined the other coven.'

Elena grew concerned. 'Why do I think that's not a good idea? He's not joining her, is he?'

Rory pursed his lips and his eyes took on a haunted expression. 'I don't know. He told me what happened, what he tried to do to you. I'm so sorry about that.' He brushed the hair from her face.

'It's not your fault. Please don't blame yourself.'

'I will always feel responsibility for him. He's my blood.'

'I know. Perhaps he'll come back one day.'

Rory shrugged. 'Maybe. He's a strange young man. He's not sorry at all for any of it. If you hadn't been his kin, he would have raped you, kept you against your will.' He lifted his shoulder and shook his head. 'I don't understand his mind.'

Neither did Elena, but she wasn't going to comment. He might be her father, but there was a lot they didn't know about each other.

'Gregor Royston said he'd try to keep Drew in hand and keep him away from your mother. She's not part of his coven, but she lives close by. I have to accept that.'

'Yes. Let's hope for the best.'

Rory nodded and tugged on his ear. 'Drew's an adult now — a fair warlock. I can't live his life for him.'

Elena nodded. 'Yes, I guess so. No, I know so. You have to live your own life now.'

They said their farewells. Elena reset the ward

and then spent an hour on the sofa, staring at her carpet. She thought the news that her mother didn't want to see her would hurt more, but she didn't feel much of anything, after the initial shock. She was more appalled that the woman dabbled in dark arts.

Her mind returned to Jake, and she thought to ring Pen in the morning.

After a restless sleep, she waited until nine a.m. and then called Jake's office. The woman was pleased to get some news. 'Thank heavens he's all right. I'm surprised, though. He's not much into family. He and his dad have a rather distant relationship, so I find it hard to believe he dropped everything for a grandfather he didn't know.'

'You know him so well.'

'We were mates at university actually — not lovers, you understand, friends. After a particularly difficult period in my life, he gave me a job. I've been here ever since. I thought I knew all there was to know about him.'

'Sometimes you think you know someone, and then they do something shocking and act out of character.'

Pen laughed. Elena could sense the relief in her. 'Yes, keeps us on our toes I suppose,' Pen said finally. Elena managed a light chuckle.

Pen assured her that she had rearranged Jake's schedule to adjust to his absence, and that he wasn't in any danger of ruining his law practice. However, next week things would get critical, as there was only so much she could do on her own.

CHAPTER TWENTY

Two nights later, there was another interference with Elena's ward. Dressed in a short nightie she crept to the door, not bothering to turn on the light. She didn't want to let on that she was home if the visitor was someone she wanted to avoid.

Hesitating before opening it, she tried to work out who it was. The vibrations were familiar, yet not. It wasn't Drew. The thought of him turning up made her heart beat faster. How many people had visited her before she'd put up her ward? Huddling by the door, she waited, all her senses on alert.

There was a rhythmic tapping on her ward perimeter, like someone was knocking. She didn't know any warlocks cheeky enough to do that. It was too strange. She opened the door a sliver, and her heart leaped. Swinging the door fully open, she took a step outside.

Under the street lamp Jake leaned against his car, his face stubbled, hands in his leather jacket. He looked relaxed and happy. Another thing she wasn't expecting. Standing there, gaping at him, she didn't even have the sense to speak.

'Hi,' he said with a rather shy grin.

Elena blinked. 'Hi.' Why did she have to be tongue-tied right then? It was a perfect opportunity to speak her mind — to tell him.

Stunned by his appearance, she didn't think to invite him in. A fact she didn't noticed until he kept talking.

'I've come on a mission.' He reached into his car and pulled out her sandals. 'I need to find the owner of these shoes. May I come in?'

'Er...yes.' Why wasn't her brain working? She had so much prepared to tell to him, and now she couldn't think of what to say. Why didn't she have her notebook handy?

Easing the ward open, she allowed him to enter. He came forward at a swift pace and she backed up. So much man heading straight at her, she did what came naturally — she let him, and got out of his way by backing herself against the wall. He came through the door and shut it behind him with a quick flick of his spare hand. The light came on.

Elena shook her head. How did that happen? Did he hit the switch on his way through?

He gestured toward the sofa with both hands, his knee bent as if bowing to her. 'If you'll take a seat, I'll see if these shoes are yours.'

With her eyes glued to him, she tried to work out what was going on. He was awfully cheerful. Finger combing her hair, she realized she looked a fright. She was in a revealing nightie. Oh dear, she had to get rid of him. 'Of course they're mine.' She held out her hand for them. 'I'll take them.'

A loud meow heralded the arrival of Fel. Making herself comfortable on one of the easy chairs, the cat tucked its front paws under its chest and wound its tail around its body. *I am not missing this.*

Elena fronted the cat, hands on hips. 'Fel go away. This is none of your business.'

'Are you talking to your cat?'

Elena swung around. 'Yes, of course I am. Now, my shoes, if you don't mind.'

He pulled them out of her reach. 'We must do this properly. Take a seat.'

Elena repressed a laugh. 'Properly?'

He kept his face composed, lifting only an eyebrow. Shaking her head, she sat down on the sofa, the shortness of her nightie leaving her knees exposed. A glance at the cat and she could see its smug expression. Her mental dart didn't make a dent in the cat's hide.

Jake knelt down with a flourish, brandishing her sandals like a bunch of flowers. He put his hand on her knee, noticing her quiver at his touch. His slid his hand down her lower leg, cupped her heel, and drew her foot out so he could slip the sandal on.

He studied her foot from both sides. 'It fits. You must be the mystery woman I'm looking for.'

'Jake?' What was he up to? She was uncertain, but her instinct told her to go along with it. Without words, was he telling her she was forgiven? Her heart leapt at the thought.

'Yet, there is another test.' He reached into his jacket and pulled out a bra, bright orange with a lace overlay. Her bra. The one she'd left on the roof top. Her face heated up. She couldn't keep eye contact.

He dangled the bra in front of her face so she had no choice but to look at it. Unable to stand the teasing, she made a grab for it, but he moved it out of her reach.

'Hey, that's my favorite bra.'

'How do I know that until I see if this garment

fits?' He quirked an eyebrow at her, forming a comic expression.

Elena didn't know what to do. How was he able to charm his way into her home, into her heart? She was not taking off her nightie to prove it was her bra. She crossed her arms over her chest and brought her chin down stubbornly.

He wiggled that eyebrow again, and she couldn't repress the giggle. Still, she didn't move her arms or relax. It wouldn't do to go along with his scheme.

'I see you are having trouble understanding me. I'm quite the expert in fitting bras. Let me help you.'

He eased his jacket off and flung it on a chair then lunged for her as she leaped sideways off the sofa, ready to head for her bedroom. Fel screeched and ran out of the room.

Not far behind, Jake caught her near the wall and turned her to face him.

His body rested against hers, all hot and lean. Elena couldn't believe she was in this situation. The hard muscles of his arms tensed as he embraced her. The thin material of her nightie wasn't much of a barrier. The way he looked at her, she could see the attraction — unadulterated attraction. He wanted her. Her eyes widened as she understood. He held her with his pelvis, and his hard erection rested against her hip.

There was no spell this time. Without words, he was saying he wanted to be there with her. A pulse beat in the heat of her sex. Obviously, she wanted him too. Her skin flushed as the arousal sped around her body, putting her cells on high alert.

'May I?' he asked softly, next to her ear. His moist, warm breath gave her goosebumps on her neck, and did all kinds of weird things to her stomach.

Elena kept her gaze on his face and nodded once.

His hands dropped to her thighs, his fingers softly caressing her. She closed her eyes at the touch of skin on skin, her nerves sizzling. Bunching her nightie up, he gathered the hem in his hands and lifted. Drawing it over her body, he sighed as she lifted her arms so it came off over her head.

Dressed only in her panties, she stood pressed up against the wall, not even daring to breathe. With great concentration, he took the bra, slid the straps over her shoulders and then asked her to turn around. Deftly, he did up the catch, and then urged her to turn again.

'Perfect,' he said in a low, husky voice that sent pleasure spiraling within her brain. Seriously, she could melt if he continued to talk to her in that way. Marveling at how his voice could exert so much control over her, she allowed herself to relax, and her arousal took over.

His eyelids were hooded, his expression still as he leaned down to slide his tongue along her lower lip, stopping to grab it gently between his teeth. The contact sent a flood of sensations through her. His passion for her rushed into her and made her gasp. This was a man of intense feeling, of deep, heartfelt love. He cared for her.

Tears threatened to ruin the moment. She held them back as she kissed him. Holding her chin, he ran his mouth across hers, slipped his tongue in and then deepened the kiss.

Elena was floating in the moment, riding it like a gentle wave. Responding to him, she sent her tongue to meet his, ran it along his teeth and then held onto the back of his neck as she thoroughly explored his mouth. She loved him. There was no doubt in her mind. The days they had been separated were like being in the desert. Drinking him in with a thirst she never thought she'd experience, she clung and let herself feel.

'Elena,' he whispered in her ear. He dropped light kisses down her neck. 'I find this so hard to believe. You want me too.'

All she could do was nod as he continued to caress her, cupping her breast and rubbing his mouth across her creamy mounds of flesh. Her nipples hardened and she ached to have him suckle them. Like he knew what she was thinking, he undid her bra and started sucking, hard. Her back arched as she was suspended between pleasure and pain. He switched breasts, sending his other hand into her panties.

She was so excited and so wet he sighed when he slid inside. He found her clitoris. Elena writhed, so overcome by his presence and the stimulating encounter. She wanted him so badly.

It was an honest want. There was no guilt, no spell, and yet it was intense. It was like she was needy, and only he could fulfill that need. She hoped that he returned the emotion. A thread of him wound into her, a subtle essence of his mind. He did feel it like she did.

'Oh Jake,' she breathed. 'I want you so bad.'

'You've got me, Elena. You've got me.' He maneuvered her so that she was lying over the arm of the sofa, her panties gone. Placing himself between her legs, his mouth came down, hot and wet as he licked her, controlling her arousal, knowing the intricacies of her body and the very pulses that made up who she was.

Elena's body was already so primed. A touch and she would fly apart. He suckled gently on her tender nub of flesh and her body jerked as her climax hit. With one hand holding her in place, Jake shucked his jeans and entered her, hard, fast, and no nonsense. Elena climaxed again. He slowed his beat, still dominating her body. He speared her with his hard erection, withdrawing the tip and then sinking in to the hilt.

Elena loved his control, loved how he mastered her. He reached down, bringing her body up. She offered him a breast and he took it, riding her at the same time. He was close to release. She grabbed his buttocks and squeezed, urging him to speed up. He understood her signal, and again she was holding on as his powerful body drove into hers. 'Come for me, baby. Come for me,' he said in her ear.

The straps of her control gave way. 'Yes,' he said. 'Yes, just like that.' He came too, a shout of joy bursting out of him.

They clung together with her butt resting on the arm of the sofa, panting as their bodies restored the balance after such a burst of emotional and physical exertion.

He nuzzled her neck and sought her lips. 'No spell this time.' He held her face in his hands and stared into her eyes. 'So much better without it.'

She lowered her lashes. 'No spell,' she agreed. He had bespelled her, with his smile, those intense eyes and his fantastic lovemaking.

'And what do you feel, little witch?'

'Feel?'

He shut his eyes and shook his head slightly. 'About me? Do I have a chance with you? Can you forgive me for the other day?'

Tears did come then, sliding silently down her cheek. 'I feel so much. I feel so much I think I'm going to explode with it. Of course I forgive you. Can you forgive me? I never meant to...'

He put his finger against her lips. 'I know. You

have proven it to me now. There is a connection be-tween us. I've never felt this way about another person in my life. I'd give you my life, if you let me.'

He wiped a tear from the corner of her eye. 'Can this be true? I never thought we'd have this moment.'

'We can have many more moments. Marry me?'

Her eyes widened. The thought frightened her. Could she commit? Witches and warlocks didn't marry, like humans. He was wanting that human bond. Yet how different was it from the first pro-posal, not much more than a week ago? This time it was so right, but could she really love on so short an acquaintance?

The skin between his eyebrows furrowed. 'Elena?'

Her hesitation was hurting him. She licked her lips. Rory had said that Elvira still loved him after all those years, and all that hurt. Could it be that way with Jake? *Yes.*

'Yes, Jake. I want to be with you.'

His face relaxed as she reached up to stroke his cheek and slide her finger along his chin. 'I love you. I want to share my life with you. If you can accept what I am.'

His lips crushed hers in a searing kiss, not wanting to let go, and then he broke for breath. 'I know what you are, Elena Denholm. I want all of you.'

Her smile was radiant. 'You can only have the parts of me I'm willing to share.'

He nipped her on the chin. 'You think?'

Elena laughed and wiped away the tears. She didn't need them anymore.

Jake carried Elena into the bedroom and lay her down carefully. The cat squealed indignantly and bounded off the bed, and ran into the spare room. Jake thought he heard the cat say something, but was too shocked by it to comment. He thought the cat said, *It's about time, tom.*

Shaking his head, he forgot about the cat, and rolled into bed beside Elena. Contentment wrapped around him like her arms as she held him. The last few days had been hell and then some, but amazing learning experiences.

Nasty leftover feelings from the spell had clung to him like cobwebs. It took a while, but Gregor fixed him so that he could see the time he'd spent with Elena without the mask of the spell.

As he held her, there was no comparison. There was none of that docile puppy love feeling or the tainted black of rejection. Despite the spell leaving him, he still wanted her, still cared for her, more than he had anyone else. It had scared him to the very core of his being. It had challenged all the beliefs he had about himself.

Light spilled in through a gap in the curtain, bringing Jake to wakefulness. His hand was resting on Elena's thigh. He was hard. He moved his hand, caressed her, and she woke a little, became receptive to making love with him. They moved together gently and sweetly, and then lay together afterwards.

'Something is different about you, Jake.' Elena propped herself on her elbow and used a forefinger to trace his stubble along his chin. Her touch sent thrills through him.

'I meant to talk to you last night, but I was a bit distracted.'

Elena smiled, her green eyes alight with merriment. 'You distracted me. Not the other way around.'

'You think so?' He chuckled, unable to repress his happiness. 'So, your father came to see me.'

Elena frowned. 'So he was who you left with on Monday? He mentioned taking you north, something about a coven.'

He lay back on the pillow and gazed at the ceiling. 'He wanted me to meet my grandfather. He happens to be a warlock.'

Elena nodded. 'Dad told me that Gregor Royston, your grandfather, had married a human and had left Sydney. He must be an interesting man to leave the coven for love.'

'You're surprised?' he said, as he turned on his side and brushed the hair off her forehead.

'That a man would give up something important for the woman he loved? A little, but you know I don't know that many warlocks, or men, for that matter.'

'I forgive you for your doubt. I wouldn't have believed it either. My father didn't have good relationships with his wives. It taught me love was all a waste of time. I was wrong.' He grinned at her. 'I like it that you don't know many warlocks or men. You won't be comparing me. I want you to learn all about me, like I want to learn all about you.'

Elena's smile lit up her eyes. 'You are dangerous and arrogant.'

He grinned at her. 'You know me too well already.'

'Anyway, so you went up north, met your grandfather and…'

'Yes, Gregor married a human. She's passed on now, though he still seems young. Handy talent, to live a lot longer than the rest of us. They had two children, my father and another son called Riley.

'I didn't meet my uncle as there was too much on. We will catch up soon. Apparently my father was all human, and didn't get on with the crowd up there. Distrusted them. Hated them, even. So Gregor set him up with money and let him go his own way. Sadly, that was the last that the old man saw of him. He kept track of him, apparently, but never made contact. It hurt the old man that my father couldn't accept him for who he was.'

'That's sad, really. From what you've said it seemed Gregor was happy to accept him as he was. What an interesting man he seems to be.'

Jake nodded and stroked the hair from her face. Their eyes met. 'And what else did you find out?' she asked, searching his face.

Pride surged up inside of him. 'I have talent, apparently. Talent I've been using all my life. Gregor assessed me and taught me stuff, too.'

'You're a warlock? I mean I knew there was something, but I…'

'Enough of a warlock for you, young lady.' He kissed her lips gently.

Laughter bubbled out of her, and Jake's heart burst to see the joy erupt from her. 'More than enough for me.'

'My prime talent is persuasion,' Jake said.

Elena laughed. 'Figures.'

'I have to learn more about it so I don't use it inadvertently in my work.' Jake loved how her eyes widened.

The phone rang. 'Ignore it,' Jake suggested.

'I can't. It's Grace. If I don't answer we'll have half the family here to investigate.' Jake watched her as she talked, loving the dimple on the side of her mouth.

'Right,' she said as she hung up. 'How fast can we shower and get dressed? They're coming!'

As they tied it in the race to the shower, they decided to double up. The water had gone cold by the time they got out. He loved how she melted when he touched her intimately. He loved the sensation of being inside her. A man could get addicted to this.

'How long do we have?' he asked as they dressed.

'Not long. I've lowered the ward.'

Jake tossed his spare condoms on the counter. 'Now I understand why you didn't get upset when the condom broke the other night. Gregor told me witches were immune to most human diseases and could fix themselves so they don't get pregnant.'

Elena gasped, and turned so her hair hid her face.

Jake's heart thumped. It wasn't good. 'What is it?'

Elena still wouldn't look at him, and her hands shook as she finger combed her hair from her face. Her eyes were dark, and there was a frown mark between her eyebrows.

'I forgot about the accident.'

'Really?' He remembered his panic with the broken condom. 'Then you could be pregnant?'

His voice came out choked. He kept telling himself he was committed to Elena, but a child? That was something that was nowhere within his radar. His own childhood had been awful. He had never wanted to inflict something similar on another human being. Elena sat on the bed, head in hands.

'Elena?'

Lifting her head, her eyes tracked his features and

tears started. Seeing her upset made him feel like such a jerk. He needed to pull himself together quickly or Elena was going to slip through his fingers. He kept his face impassive.

She shook her head, trying to appear calm, but he could see the telltale signs of stress, the swallowing, the clenching of her hands, the pale hue of her skin. 'Goddess,' she said. 'I've been so preoccupied I haven't been paying attention to my own body. I'll get Grace to check me over. Perhaps she can fix it.'

Penderton had told him about how desperate the coven was for children to be born to those with talent. How could he even hint or suggest that Elena should abort any potential child when there was that pressure on her? He thought maybe, when they were more established, they could try for a child. He ran his fingers through his hair. He had no idea what to think. He was stonkered.

Yet, he had to act and act right. 'No. If there's a baby I don't want you to fix it.' Jake's eyes widened. Had those words come out of his mouth? Yes, and they felt right, too. His heart may be beating rather irregularly, but deep down he knew this was right. He wanted Elena, and everything that went with her.

Elena looked up and wiped a tear away. Her chin rose. 'It's okay, Jake. I understand. If I'm pregnant and it's too late to stop it then I'll look after the child by myself. I'm quite capable.' Her gaze locked on the wall, and her hands screwed up the bed sheet. Compassion welled up in him. He would be silly to let his inner wimp lose him this wonderful woman. They would have a child, most likely a child with talent. Together they would explore this strange new world of parenthood and witchery.

He knelt on the floor beside her and took her hand. 'Elena. It will be fine. I'm here for you. Whatever that means in the future.' He shrugged. 'Be it your extended family, or a family of our own.'

She threw her head back and her gaze traveled over his face, her lips pursed. He smiled at her. 'I am sorry about it.'

He reached out and ran his palm over the back of her head. 'Accidents happen. We have to deal with the consequences.' *No matter how scary*, he thought. He breathed in, deep. Elena was oblivious to his inner turmoil; or at least, he hoped she was.

Elena kissed him lightly. 'We better get dressed,' she said, as she reached for a floral sundress and slipped it over her head. Jake reached for his jeans.

As she straightened her hair and applied some lip gloss, Elena said, 'Last night we didn't use protection either. So you have the immunity of the folk?'

He grinned at her. 'Yes, and the longevity. We can have a long life together.'

'Elena?' It was Aunt Elvira popping in, luckily calling her from the living room. A talented witch, yet her timing sucked. No one was perfect, Elena supposed.

CHAPTER TWENTY-ONE

Elena raced into the living room and straight into her aunt's embrace. 'Oh, Aunt.'

'You can call me mother from now on, dearest.'

'Mother?'

'Yes, Rory and I have decided to commit to a life together.'

The door opened, and in walked her father. He did not have Elvira's talent to lope in through walls unannounced. Elena glanced between them and took in Rory's very wide grin. He nodded, confirming Elvira's news.

'But what about…?' Elena would hate to offend her best friend, cousin, and adopted sister by presuming to call her mother her own.

'Grace is fine with it. She'll be here in a minute. She's bringing Declan. He's finally arrived back after riding that infernal motorbike up to the Blue Mountains.'

There was a sound of movement behind her. Jake was heading her way. Rory stepped forward. 'I see that Jake turned up.'

Her father introduced Jake to Elvira. The old

witch looked him up and down, her lips pursed, and then she grinned, a gleam in her eye. Jake's eyebrows rose and his cheeks turned pink. He'd have to get used to Aunt Elvira. She was a powerful witch, and that was unsettling for all of them at times.

Elena had the grace to blush as Jake's intense blue eyes fired up her arousal. She had to control herself. Elvira's gaze rested on her. Elena couldn't stop the color that stole up her face and neck. Elvira nodded knowingly, and then clasped Rory's hand.

It was odd having a man in her life, and as much as she loved her family, it was difficult having them knowing what she was doing and also knowing what she was thinking and feeling. After a wink at her, Rory went to shake Jake's hand. 'So, are congratulations in order?'

Jake slapped him on the back. 'You bet, old man.'

Elena shuddered. Surely they didn't mean that she might be pregnant. She relaxed, realizing they meant that she and Jake had sorted things out between them.

'Hey none of that. I'll be Dad to you. We're a real family here.'

They shared a look. Jake looked down at their joined hands. 'Sure. Dad sounds great.'

Elena glanced between them. 'You knew,' she accused her father, 'and you didn't tell me?'

He held up his hands and backed away. 'Now, love, he made me promise. I told you it was his story to tell.'

Grace knocked on the door, bringing with her the handsome Declan. He was slightly taller than Jake, and seriously challenged his hunk status. Declan surged over to Elena, picked her up and swung her around. 'I'm so happy for you.' He put her down and kissed her forehead. 'I'm so sorry I wasn't here when you needed me. Grace tells me you went through the wringer.'

Elena ran her fingers through her hair, feeling a bit embarrassed. 'A little. Come and meet Jake.'

Jake and Declan looked each other up and down. Jake put his hand out with a grin.

'Nice to meet Grace's man, finally. She's a lovely woman. Took good care of me when I was... well...vulnerable.'

Grace sidled up next to her mate and put her arms around his waist, her smile wide. 'It was a pleasure. You make great coffee, and provided a great deal of good conversation. You're wonderful for Elena, too. I've never seen her look so happy, so contented.'

Jake's cheeks turned pink. Elena hid a smile behind her hand. He'd have to deal with her loving but intrusive family, too. It would be hard for a single child who'd been brought up isolated in a boarding school. If he could manage it, she certainly could too.

He seemed to cope well, given the little discussion they had about the accident. Elena was afraid — she feared losing him, and potentially being a mother.

'I have news for you,' Jake said to Grace. 'My client liked your proposal and it's a deal. The papers will go through soon, as well as the settlement. That eco park idea of yours was exactly what the development needed. Well done.'

Grace shared a look with Elena. 'Maybe I could consult for you sometime.'

'Sure. I'm all for good ideas. Won't you be rather busy?' He indicated her swollen belly.

'I have a very healthy man to help me look after our child. I believe I also have babysitters.' She looked meaningfully at Elena and Jake.

Jake put his arm around Elena's shoulder. 'Sure,

anytime.' Elena smiled, loving that Jake was getting into the family groove, although he and Grace had always clicked.

Later as they sat around the living room, Grace handed out some red wine. 'Don't give any to Elena,' Elvira said.

Grace stood up with the tray in hand. 'Why?'

Elvira sniffed. 'She's expecting.'

Elena gasped, and her hand went to her abdomen. Surely one mistake couldn't result in a baby. She didn't know if she could look at Jake. Yet the sound of him choking on red wine brought her around to face him, heart thudding, paralyzed with fear.

Rory pounded him on the back. When Jake recovered, he asked, 'How can you tell? It's too soon.' His voice was barely audible.

Elvira looked down her nose at him. 'I'm a witch. These things are easy to detect. She's expecting. Early days yet, but no wine for Elena.'

Elena was sure she was going to faint. Elvira grasped her hand and squeezed. 'It will be fine, my dear. You have all of us here for you both. What a lovely thing for the coven, for Rory and me. Grandparents together.'

Without speaking, her father stood up and headed to the bathroom. 'What are you doing, Rory?' Elvira asked, turning in her seat to face him, and letting go of Elena's hand.

He paused and faced them all and shrugged. 'Just getting a cold compress.'

'What on earth for? You're perfectly well.'

Rory nodded. 'I am, but Jake looks like he's going to faint.'

Concerned, Elena went over to him, her eyes narrowing. 'Are you okay?"

They shared a look and he gave a single nod.

Trembling, Elena squeezed in next to him. He hugged her, and then kissed her forehead. 'We will be fine,' he said, though his voice was still croaky. There had been a moment when he'd panicked, when they discussed the accident in the bedroom. That was when their relationship hung in the balance, but Jake had come through. At that moment, he just looked surprised, and as uncertain as she was.

Elena noticed the quiet first, and looked around at her family. They were all staring at Jake, and then she noticed his pale face. Her family burst out laughing. Rory tossed the wet towel at him, which Jake used to wipe his face and neck with exaggerated movements. When he was done, he gave them a lopsided smile and a shrug of his shoulders. 'I've never been expecting before.'

Elena smiled at his words. When he looked into her face, Jake's expression was intense and full of love. Happiness filled Elena to the brim.

Jake lifted her onto his lap, gave her a peck on the lips and then nuzzled her neck.

'Me neither,' Elena said and hugged him.

THE END

ACKNOWLEDGEMENTS 2014

I'd like to thank Romance Writers of Australia for inspiring me to write this romance. The idea came to me at the end of the August 2012 conference and was so hot in my mind that I wrote the outline on the way home from Brisbane. I wrote on the train, in the airline lounge, and on the plane. Romance Writers of Australia provides a fabulous annual convention with excellent professional development for writers. Those guys rock.

Also, I'd like to thank my friend Elizabeth Dunk, for her amazing and useful critique. Kate Cuthbert, my editor, is an awesome woman. *Bespelled* wouldn't be published without her patience and her support. Thanks, Kate, for your faith in me.

To my wonderful partner, Matthew, I want to say thank you for your love and writing conversations.

Last, but not least, a big thank you to the gang at the Canberra Speculative Fiction Guild for being there, and offering great support for writers.

ACKNOWLEDGEMENTS 2019

It is with great pleasure that I bring Bespelled to you to read. I have the rights back and so I have control over the publication process, the covers, the marketing and so on.

Bespelled was my very first paranormal romance publication. I've gone on to do more, but this is the first and a real joy. The idea just burned out of me in a big rush. However, it took lot of work from my editor to get it right.

I love how I was able to bring my love of the Balmain area into a story. I've not lived there myself, but visited often after I moved to Canberra. It was just the kind of place I think a witches' coven would choose as it is close to the water, and quirky in a very nice way.

Dani
November 2019

ABOUT THE AUTHOR

Dani Kristoff is a Canberra-based author, who delights in reading and writing paranormal romance. She's been writing since late 2000, which means nearly twenty years, although she's been concentrating her efforts on science fiction, fantasy and horror. Published both traditionally and independently, she's currently undertaking a PhD in creative writing at the University of Canberra. Her research area is feminism and romance. Her partner is also a writer and they get up to geekery whenever possible.